Hmmm?

A TALE OF MYSTERIOUS MURRR-DERRR AND A GIRL

SIMON PLASTER

 Published by Mossik Press.

mossikpress@mail.com

Library of Congress Cataloguing-in-Publication Data

Plaster, Simon [7.19.2016]

Hmmm?

by Simon Plaster

p. cm

ISBN 978-0-991-4480-6-7

1. Humor—Fiction.

2. Oklahoma, United States—Fiction.

3. Mystery—Fiction.

4. Noir—Fiction.

I. Title1

0 9 8 7 6 5 4 3 2 1

Manufactured in the United States of America

First Edition

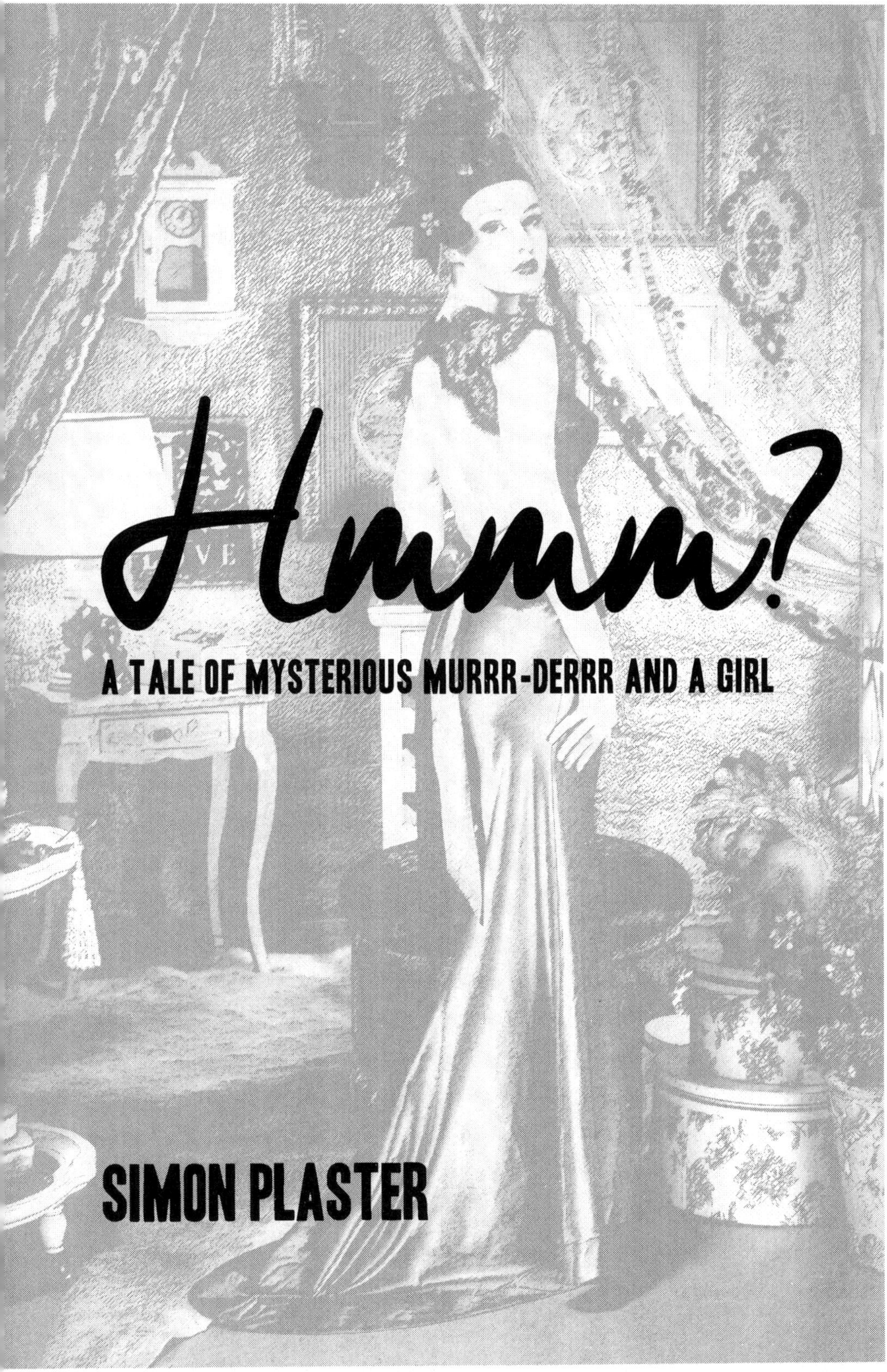

Hmmm?

A TALE OF MYSTERIOUS MURRR-DERRR AND A GIRL

SIMON PLASTER

HENRYETTA WEEKLY HERALD

Henryetta, OK

03 / 01 / 2016

LOCAL DEATHS

R.I.P.

Lehough, A. - age unknown, died February 29, 2016. Cause of death: A mystery. Services extremely private.

OKMULGEE TRIBUNE

Okmulgee, OK

02 / 11 / 2016

PERSONALS

R.S.V.P.

Man seeks Woman for Valentine's Day hot time.
Reply: Lehough, P.O. Box 2020, Henryetta, OK

One

Since changing the legal spelling of her name—putting an i where her mother, Wynona Sue, wrote a y on her birth certificate twenty-some years before—Henrietta had not noticed much improvement in her life. She was still stuck in the same old rut: Still living in the little ol' Oklahoma town she was originally named for. Still not getting an exciting big city newspaper job to replace her usually tedious employment at the *Henryetta Weekly Herald*. And still not getting over Gaylord Goodhart, the love of her life, who long ago—in her mother's old fashioned term for being rejected by the one you wanted— gave her the mitten. But now she was at least hopeful for a brighter future, such as advertised in a brochure sent to her from Murray State University. Eager as a bird dog to get started, Henrietta looked at a wall clock across the P's-n-Q's pool hall and quaint cafe from where she sat, and counted off another minute.

In her not so bright past, she had earned only a half-semester credit in Remedial Reading and Writing before dropping out of Murray State to look after her mother, Wynona Sue, who at the time was recovering from a brain stroke brought on by a broken heart and likely also by cigarette smoking. Her mother had soon got back to being alive-and-well, though still clingy as ever, but now Henrietta's alma mater offered online courses that working gals like her could take without having to be on campus over in Tishomingo. She had enrolled in a two-week English Department introductory course about *The Classic Love Story: An examination of literature's same old narrative of passion, jealousy and hate.* Last night she studied up on the first and second chapters of *Genesis* in her grandma's old Bible. Today's first online lecture was scheduled to start at one o'clock and—Henrietta again looked over at the wall clock—dang it, she was sure to be tardy.

On the phone earlier, her mother said she had something to tell that "couldn't wait," but already Wynona Sue was almost twenty minutes late, probably detained by a troublesome tint-and-perm job at The Best Little Hair House in Town—where she worked—that might have her tangled up for hours in dark roots and loose ends if...Wynona Sue rushed to the table, hollered at a waiter to bring two glasses of white wine, and set down.

"Henrietta, you will never guess who has smitten me," she said, breathing heavy as a new bride on the first night of a honeymoon. "And the feeling is mutual, quite mutual, I must say."

Hmmm? That was a hard one that could take a whole day of guessing, and likely then some, Henrietta reckoned. Wynona Sue was inclined to fall in love with any and every man who gave her a tumble. For years after getting her heart broke, again and again, her mother would now and then refer to one or another of the heartbreakers—not including Henrietta's long gone Cajun daddy—as having been "the love of her life." So the possibilities of who it was that had lately smitten her were numerous as fleas on a mangy dog.

"Alexander Lehough!" her chronical lovestruck mother announced, beaming like a school girl who'd just got her first kiss.

Henrietta was stunned down to her sneakers. She had done a lot of newspaper reporting about Professor Lehough—pronounced Lee-ho—who was, well, not the type of man she could imagine even Wynona Sue getting smitten by, and vice versa. He worked at home for the Oklahoma State University Extension Services Bureau, and knew about everything there was to know out of a book. Odd facts about insects were his particular interest, but as for romancing a gal…that was strange to picture as socks on a rooster.

"He happened to come into the Hair House this morning, and I noticed right away he was <u>not</u> wearing a wedding ring, not anymore." A wicked smile crossed Wynona Sue's made-up face. "As you know, his wife…his <u>ex</u>-wife… is that brunette hussy who ran off with Virgil Carter," her mother said, before grabbing a glass out of their waiter's hand and gulping down a mouthful of white wine. A couple of years ago, Virgil Carter, a smooth talking door-to-door pots and pans salesman who semi-accidentally got nominated to run for Vice-President of the United States, was a love of Wynona Sue's life. But then her mother and Professor Lehough, by coincidence, had ended up as the odd ones out of two interlocking love triangles. So it seemed double odd that somehow…

"I recognized the name Lehough in a… from a recent interesting article in the *Okmulgee Tribune,* and well remembered Alex of course from that high-society Tick Ball in Oklahoma City: Square dancing with that stuck-up big-city socialite unfortunately, while I was stuck in a do-si-do with Virgil."

Henrietta her own self now recalled the sight of bugs flying out of the professor's longish hair and walrus mustache as his lanky body twitched on the dance floor in semi-rhythm with a lively fiddle tune. They, the bugs, were ticks as it turned out, one of which later crawled down the low-cut front of his dance partner's ball gown. The professor was set on saving the state's tick population from climate change back then, and later won a big... Well, he got a semi-big scientific prize for his "Lone Star Tick and Alfa Gal" theory for how to lower global warming. According to Professor Lehough, ticks, unlike fireflies and buryin' beetles and...

"Alex happened to drop in, to hunt for cockroaches," Wynona Sue continued. "Cockroaches dine on human hair, you know, which is high in proteins. They are more intelligent than some people think, they can be trained to do tricks, and they make wonderful pets. Seeing Alex on his hands and knees at my feet, mumbling softly, coaxing them out of baseboard cracks, I began to think of him as a lot like Robert Redford in..."

Robert Redford!

"... you know, in that old movie about whispering to horses. He, Alex, needed a haircut in the worst way, so..." As her mother went on to tell about getting Professor "Alex" into her chair and going to work on his shaggy hair and mustache, Henryetta again looked at the wall clock. According to the Murray State course catalogue, "The Classic Love Story" involved a mystery that would test the detective wits of even Sherlock Holmes. Despite Wynona Sue's romance record that would make her a likely victim, or suspect, in about any real-life version of any tale of "passion, jealousy and hate," how she and Professor Lehough got mutually smitten really was a stumper. On the other hand, Henrietta had heard that love was blind.

"Most men tend to look sort of goofy with bangs, but Alex... Looking at each other in the beauty parlor wall mirror, our eyes met," her mother said in a dreamy sort of way. "Something passed between us, and Alex—in that bashful, mumbly way of his—asked if he could have, well, not exactly a lock of my hair, but any eyebrow pluckings that might fall beside my chair, which was sweet. His pet hissing cockroaches from Madagascar love eyebrows and lashes. For special occasions he much prefers them to commercial roach jellies. I thought it might seem too, uh, forward of me to invite him to pay a social call tomorrow evening, which is Valentine's Day, you know. So he's dropping by the house tonight for Friendly Creature highballs," her mother said, while running a finger across one of her own well groomed eyebrows, "and perhaps—I made no promises—for some plucking."

After hightailing it back to her desk in the *Weekly Herald's* storefront office, where she had already put two sharp pencils next to an opened spiral notebook, Henrietta fired up her computer and went to class, but dang it...

Professor LeRoy:

So in conclusion, yes, the first story of romantic love between Man and Woman goes back to Adam and Eve in the Garden of Eden. We sense having once been whole with another, and yearn to be reunited with a lost part of ourselves. Any questions?

Agnetta Hurley:

You mean like me and Bobo both signed the apartment lease, and since he moved out he don't pay his half of the rent?

Professor LeRoy:

Well, I suppose one could say that in the eyes of the all-powerful "LandLORD" (lol)—and perhaps yours too, Ms. Hurley—you and Bobo legally were and remain a "one," that cannot and should not be put asunder (lol).

Agnetta Hurley:

Our shoes and socks never got sorted out neither. We have the same size feet, which was one, actually four things we had in common.

Barbara Jean Booker:

Cry me a river. I donated a kidney to my ex and he won't give it back. It's out there every night, hanging out with "the boys." Soaking up beer and having a ball while I sit at home, pissed, to put it mildly.

Professor LeRoy:

Yes, well, one might say your former kidney is like Adam's rib, in a sense: a part of you that is now part of your ex. I am sure he thinks of you fondly, Ms. Booker, probably every night. And may someday feel drawn back to that other lost part of himself that is his "mate."

Barbara Jean Booker:

In our family Bible, Lilith was Adam's first wife. She refused to lay down in the Missionary Position and divorced him.

Professor LeRoy:

Another story stemming from another rib, perhaps (lol).

Barbara Jean Booker:

No, she came first. The goddess Maya made "Adam" out of one of Lilith's body parts.

Professor LeRoy:

Let me guess (lol). A kidney, right?

Dang it! 'Cause of being late to class and missing the first part of Professor LeRoy's lecture, Henrietta was confused as a goat on shag carpet, but too embarrassed of her ignorance to butt in and type something dumb.

Two

At a lavatory in the bathroom of his Division Street bungalow, lathering up his cheeks for a shave, Professor Alexander Lehough hardly recognized the already well groomed man in the mirror as his true, still youthful self: "Alex." *Ah yes, the would be Prince Charming returns to the joust*, said the inner voice of his alter ego, whom he thought of as "Zander." *At fifty-odd years of age, you look like a pathetic schoolboy, Alex, getting yourself all shined up to go a-courtin'. Is that a pimple I see on your chin? Is awkward adolescence again raising its ugly head?* Despite himself, Alex gently dabbed a foamy finger on a reddish spot that slightly marred his appearance. "How would you know about 'adolescence'?" he muttered in reply. "You, Zander, are a classic case of arrested development, still as hopelessly childish as the day we met." *And you, Alex, are still a dork, as clueless as you were when we were teenagers. Only one woman answers your pathetic newspaper ad and you think* <u>*you're*</u> *gonna score tonight. Hmmm? Remember that time in junior high school when you tried to get Louellorene Corker to kiss your pet "reptile"?*

"We were Biology lab partners, dissecting a frog, and Louellorene Corker was a little flirt," Alex protested. *Yeah, she only wanted to make her real boyfriend jealous, as I recall, and it worked. "Knuckles" Fricke de-pants you on the schoolyard and little "Sir Hiss" became a laughing stock.* "Louellorene told me she wished I could be her 'Prince Charming'. I naturally thought..." *Uh-huh, you just played along with the fairy tale; just like you did this morning when you let that strawberry blonde "plucker" believe you had won a Nobel Prize for coming up with a solution for so-called global warming.*

That was a low blow, even by the increasingly juvenile Trumpian standards of Zander's recent sniping. Though a climate change skeptic himself, he, Alex, had served as an expert witness in a class action lawsuit brought by an association of Oklahoma ranchers and farmers, aggrieved by urban-based production of CO2. But only for the higher cause of saving *your unhappy marriage to...* No! He had testified in court on the side of the ranchers and farmers to help win a monetary judgement that would save the rural deer population, upon which the survival of ticks depended, *while hoping desperately—but alas, in vain—to win back the affections of your wife, What's-Her-name, that were fixated on that pots-and-pans huckster, Virgil Carter.* Not necessarily. Carter's illustrated sales spiel on behalf of the environment—comparing greenhouse gases to the lid of a leadware pot and the planet to an overcooked ham hock—had made him a hero to many well intentioned worriers, *no doubt including many other sexually frustrated women.*

Whatever. From the witness stand, he, Alex, had simply informed the judge and jury that agriculture—mainly through belching and farting livestock, along with massive production of manure—generated vast quantities of methane gas that contributed more than fossil fuel combustion to the so-called "greenhouse effect" that supposedly caused global warming. For his "Lone Star Tick and Alfa Gal Theory," offering a scientifically sound solution to the so-called problem, he was later awarded *not the Nobel Prize for saving the planet, but the freaking Noble Oil Company Prize for screwing up the farmers' and ranchers' case and saving, not any deer herds and ticks, but ongoing fossil fuel consumption and the company's corporate profits!*

"Dog gone it, the Nobel/Noble mix-up was a misprint in the headline of a *New York Times* article sent in by Miss Wynona Sue's own daughter, a local newspaper reporter who covered the trial. What was I to do, tell a proud mother about the *Times'* follow-up front page retraction blaming the foul-up on her daughter, calling the young woman an idiot, and worse? The Associated Press had already spread the misinformation way beyond anyone's ability to take it back." *You didn't take back the wife either,* Zander persisted in reminding him, *who was, as they say a "real prize." No, she didn't withdraw her demand for a divorce that I recall. In fact, she showed up at the courthouse during that trial and...*

Having covered all but the mustachioed upper lip of the bewhiskered portions of his face with foam, Alex sought to drown out further Zander commentary by beginning to sing under his breath as he shaved: "Froggie went a-courtin' and he did ride, uh-huh/ Froggie went a-courtin' and he did ride, uh-huh/ Froggie went a-courtin' and he did ride..."

You discredited Virgil Carter and his "Oscar worthy" slide show misrepresentation of science, but...

"He took Wynona Sue upon his knee, uh-huh/ He took Wynona Sue upon his knee, uh-huh/ He took Wynona Sue upon his knee/ Said 'Miss Wynona Sue, will you marry me?'

Uh-huh."

Marriage? Alex, really, don't you think you're getting perhaps a teeny-weeny bit ahead of yourself?

"What should the wedding supper be? Uh-huh/ What should the wedding supper be? Uh-huh/ What should the wedding supper be?/ Fried mosquito and black-eyed pea, uh-huh/ And first to come was a flyin' moth, uh-huh/ First to come was a flyin' moth, uh-huh/ First to come was a flyin' moth/ Wynona Sue laid out the table cloth, uh-huh."

Yep, "The Lone Star Tick," so to speak, ran Carter out of town alright. Ruined your romantic rival's door-to-door pots-and-pans sales business. But the wife, 'Alfa Gal', so to speak, ran out of town with Virgil, didn't she, Alex?

"Next to come in was a broken-back flea, uh-huh/ Next to come in was a broken-back flea, uh-huh/ Next to come in was a broken-back flea/ Danced a jig with the bumbley bee, uh huh."

Now that I think of it, didn't your new ladylove once upon a time also have a...a romantic relationship with Virgil Carter?

"Ouch!" Somewhat distracted by Zander's unchivalrous reference to Miss Wynona Sue's past, Alex had nicked his chin. A minor cut, barely broke the skin, nothing to spoil his mood. "Next to come in was a little black tick, uh-huh/ Next to come in was a little black tick, uh-huh/ Next to come in was a little black tick/ She ate so much she made us sick, uh-huh."

Any chit-chat between you and "Miss Wynona Sue" about your own marital past, future intentions, or for that matter...?

"No, the subject didn't expressly come up," Alex mumbled into a towel as he wiped remnants of foam from his face. "We talked only of our shared enthusiastic interest in cockroaches. I'm taking a few prize hissers on our date."

How romantic. Reminds me of the moonlit night you pitched woo to the first wife. Ah yes, lying together in a grassy field, looking up to a sky devoid of stars but filled with fireflies, you informed her that the twinkling light came out of the fireflies' anuses. That sealed the deal alright. She plighted her troth to Sir Hiss, so to speak, only to later kiss the pet "reptile" of another, namely that of Virgil Carter who in fact did turn into her prince.

That did it. Alex opened a medicine cabinet above the bathroom lavatory. There he found a brown bottle containing a powerful potion he'd concocted for dealing with Zander when all else failed.

And by the way, Alex, did you ever get any document making it official that the wife actually got around to divorcing you? I myself don't recall ever seeing...

Alex took a dangerously big swig of the potent potion, and immediately...*No, Alex, please, no! You're killing me!* A deathly quiet fell.

Moments later, satisfied that his disagreeable "other self" was dead to the world, Alex uncapped another bottle and splashed his face with an extra strong dose of *Old Spice* aftershave lotion. Again, he admired his new well-groomed look in the bathroom mirror and went back to singing beneath his breath: "Next to come was a little green snake, uh-huh/ Next to come was a little green snake, uh-huh/ Next to come was a little green snake/ Ate up all the wedding cake, uh-huh."

From a cabinet below the lavatory, Alex then retrieved a cardboard box containing several hissing cockroaches and—feeling somewhat under the influence of the powerful potion he'd administered to Zander—set out with slightly staggering steps for Miss Wynona Sue's modest little house on nearby Trudgeon Street.

"Froggie went a-courtin and he did ride, uh-huh/ Froggie went a courtin' and he did ride, uh-uh/ Froggie went a-courtin' and he did ride..."

Three

After working all morning at her *Weekly Herald* desk, editing the week's *Police Log* feature, writing up other local news—plus reading all her prior newspaper stories about Professor Lehough—Henrietta drove her old yellow Checker cab of a car home for lunch. Seated at a pink formica table in the kitchenette of her singles-only Shangri-La apartment, set on learning about the mystery of classic love stories in old books, she fired up her laptop and went to class:

Professor LeRoy:

On the off chance anyone found last night's episode of Keeping Up With The Kardashians even more entertaining than the assigned reading of Plato, I shall briefly re-cap what Aristophanes had to say in The Symposium about the nature of love between, in particular, Man and Woman, to-wit: Originally, the sexes were not two, but three: male, female, and an androgynous union of both sexes. All humans were composed of two equal parts joined back to back like Siamese twins, with two heads, four arms and four legs. Any of this ring a bell?

Charlie Morrison:

Is class over?

Professor LeRoy:

Not quite yet, Charlie. I was harkening back to yesterday's story in the first chapter of Genesis, to-wit: "God created man in his own image...male and female he created them. Hmmm?"

Charlie Morrison:

Is that a question at me?

Professor LeRoy:

Back to Aristophanes' version of the classic love story: Terrible was the might and great were the thoughts in the hearts of two-part mankind, so much so that they challenged the supremacy of the gods, especially that of Zeus, who was not amused. "Methinks I have a plan which will humble their pride and improve their manners," he said, before cutting each and every human being in two, like apples halved for pickling. So the androgynous kind became separate Man and Woman!

Ding dong! Is anybody still here?

Charlie Morrison:

Is this class in audio? No bells are ringing for me, Professor.

Professor LeRoy:

The point is that Aristophanes' tale is essentially the same old story as first told in the Book of Genesis! Out of androgynous Adam, God took the female part and thereby created both Man and Woman! And if the Bible version is not understood by everyone as the classic love story, Aristophanes makes it clear, to-wit: "Each of us when separated is always looking for our other half. Men who are a section of that double nature which was a union of male-and-female are lovers of women, and vice versa." And as we shall see, this story repeats itself over and over in literature, and in real life.

Charlie Morrison:

The way I read it, the storyteller—What's-His-Name—was drunk, at a stag party with some buddies, making fun of girly stuff about love.

Agnetta Hurley:

Yeah, they were all drunk, hanging out in some private "gentlemen's club," bullshitting back and forth about sex. Like all guys do.

Barbara Jean Booker:

And they were all gay. The "girly stuff"— souls yearning to be welded back into one "as the very expression of a sensed ancient need"—was all about the same-sex humans who were sliced into homo and lesbo fruits.

Professor LeRoy:

Correct. But this course is about the classic love story of Man and Woman as told in the historical and cultural mainstream of literature. As for Aristophanes and his buddies being intoxicated, well: In Vino Veritas (lol).

Charlie Morrison:

Are you shit-faced, Professor? Kinda early in the day, huh?

Agnetta Hurley:

And you're sexist, which is worse. I'm going to tell on you to Dean Rottweiler.

Barbara Jean Booker:

Drunk, sexist, homophobic, no doubt hateful toward transgender urinators and probably a Republican carnivore! I, for one, am offended by your hurtful triggers.

Though she remained quiet about it, Henrietta her own self also felt semi-offended and hurt. After Gaylord gave her the mitten, she'd had a hard time believing he was truly gay. For years she held onto the notion they would get back together, like two halves of an apple about to get pickled. Even after she her own self stood next to Gaylord six months ago—as "best man" at the wedding of him and his Dallas Cowboy teammate, Billy Ray Williams—she had kept on believing that he was still and would always be "the love of her life." Now, thanks to already getting over-educated by Professor LeRoy—dang him!—she understood that the two of them had been only a mismatched apple-and-orange that couldn't have been really in love.

Barbara Jean Booker:

College is supposed to be a safe place, LeRoy. We're going to stage a protest and shut up your love speech for good!

Henrietta closed the laptop with a sigh and got up from the pink formica table. At a counter, making a baloney sandwich, she recalled her wise old Cajun grandma telling her that out there somewhere was a lid for every pot, and vice versa. With that hopeful thought in mind, she went to a shelf of books in her living room, found the one she wanted, and plopped into an easy chair. Munching on the sandwich, she then commenced to thumb through the high school yearbook. Immediately—though embarrassed by the recollection—she recalled Wynona Sue telling her at the beginning of tenth grade to "get one of the good ones before the other girls get 'em all," meaning she should start "putting out" to one of the varsity football players. She tried, but being shortish, still nearly flat-chested, semi-freckled and semi-redheaded, well, at the time she didn't much care for boys anyway. Not until the next year, when she first laid eyes on Gaylord…

Henrietta bit her tongue and held firm to focusing on the way things were the year before she "got pretty" enough to become a cheerleader and member of the in-crowd her own self. Most of that bunch—big-breasted gals and wide-in-the-shoulders, narrow-between-the-eyes varsity jocks— got married to their "steadies" weeks before and after graduation, which had always been common practice in the little ol' town of Henryetta, Oklahoma. And no doubt lots of them were already divorced and back to being single, but...Henrietta turned a page and commenced to re-appraise nerdy boys in the Senior Class who had likely not yet found a pot to set on:

Merle "Motor Mouth" Mathews...semi-cute in the face but way shorter than even her, and no doubt completely bald by now... *Debate Club Member...most likely to become a lawyer.*

Albert "Bertie" Mettenbaugh...neck skinny as a fiddle string back then...*Body Building Club Member*...apparently not most likely to become anything but muscular.

Otto "Otto" Stack...no picture...no extracurricular activities listed...*Most likely to become an assistant librarian.*

Mort "Smelly" Williams...uh huh, he looked the part... *Class Horndog...Member of Barnacle Bill's Barbershop Quartet... Most likely to asphyxiate someone with way too much Old Spice cologne.*

Henrietta moved on to the Junior Class boys:

Butch "Walter" Bernard...a younger, thinner semi-lookalike of an old TV character with bangs called Captain Kangaroo, who Wynona Sue thought was her own daddy when she was young...*Boy Scout Troop Member...Band Member (cymbals)... Bird Club Member...Chess Club Member...Veterinary Dental Club Member ...Nature Club Member...Pets Club Member...Science Club Member...Taxidermy Club Founder & President*...almost blind, to judge by the coke-bottle glasses he wore in high school, but not unbearable to look at...*Most likely to never find time (or willing girl) for marriage.*

Semi-recalling "Walter" as semi-likable in a dorky way, Henrietta made a mental note to get back to his page, then skipped through the rest of that class to hers, though she already knew that wettin' a line in that particular puddle was likely a waste of time. Sure enough, only one of her classmates even semi-passed an eyeball test:

Jackson "Knot Hole" Malloy...who had a wide-eyed but not so innocent look of a window peeper, which he was known to be... *Locker Rooms Proctor...Most likely to get arrested some day.*

Henrietta closed the yearbook and again sighed like a virgin. Her Cajun grandma, she now recalled, also said that scratching the initials of the one you wanted on a lump of sugar would lead to true love. And as she her own self already knew for a fact, that didn't work no better than burning a pink candle for nine straight days!

Four

Through a fly-specked window of a dingy house trailer parked in the middle of a desolate area of east Texas, Charlene Lehough a/k/a "Jenny Cooper" looked out upon a landscape as bleak as her once romantic relationship with Virgil Carter had become. In the background, a radio played evocative Golden Oldies. A housefly circled her short, spiked, heavily moussed platinum blonde hair. Almost five years ago, married to that mumbling doofus, Alex, she fell for Virgil, not at first sight exactly, but only minutes after he appeared at the front door of that bug-infested bungalow in Henryetta, Oklahoma she shared with her hopelessly unromantic husband. "What's the one thing every woman wants that'll last forever?" he asked, before barging in with what turned out to be a complimentary cake knife in one hand and a large satchel of *Everlasting Leadware* samples dangling from the other. "A new kitchen appliance? Uh-uh, mechanical equipment wears out over time, and so does true love, by the way. But <u>not</u> your gran'ma's old skillet!" he said, producing a frying pan from the battered suitcase. "'Cause it was made to last, and only gets better for fryin' over time. Aint that right, Missy?"

She had been not at all interested in Virgil's line of pots and pans "guaranteed to outlive her," nor initially in him, even though he was redheaded. Not until he announced he was running for Okmulgee County Commissioner as that rarest of bird or fowl in Oklahoma—a true Democrat—did her heart begin to flutter.

Wise men say/ only fools rush in/ but I can't help falling in love...

Charlene swatted the pesky housefly with a rolled-up newspaper and tried, unsuccessfully, to dismiss from her mind bitter memory of the heartbreak that followed the first round of her tumultuous love affair with Virgil Carter. She took him, a political novice, under her radically liberal left wing. Overnight he became a "darling," not only to her, to the national news media. But even before he was picked to run for Vice-President on the national ticket, she discovered, alas, that Virgil was a chick magnet, mutually irresistible to not only her but to countless other women. *Should I stay?/ Would it be a sin*? Elvis crooned

By then she was hopelessly hooked on Virgil. While every other no-good man she had ever known only wanted—not to get into her pants—to get into her dirty mind, Virgil respected her for her body.

Though a tear had failed to materialize in either of her brown eyes, Charlene nevertheless wiped a cheek with her hand, lit a joint, and continued to silently sing her own sad sob song. She blamed Alex for Virgil's loss of the semi-Oval Office; for her loss of the near certainty of joining him as Second Lady in the off-White House; and for...She swiveled on her perch, reached into a refrigerator for a bottle of beer, and visually searched the house trailer's small kitchenette for another creepy creature to murder. Devastated to have been rejected by voters, and no doubt too ashamed to face her, Virgil disappeared immediately after the election. Worried sick that he, like Romeo, might kill himself in heartbroken despair, Charlene had set out to the farthest reaches of civilization, and beyond, in desperate quest to find...

A plume of dust appeared in the wake of a vehicle on the mile-long dirt road leading into the innermost bowels of the Flying Feathers Ranch, where Charlene now lived in constant fear of herself being found. She tossed the joint, put the beer bottle and newspaper on a counter, reached for a handy shotgun, and crouched below the dirty window.

Just as Elvis had warned: Fools in love rushed in where angels feared to tread. Over a period of more than two years, her search for Virgil took her to countless out-of-the-way places she would not otherwise have dared to enter: A Mexican border town, Nuevo Laredo, where she was forced to find lodging in a cheap brothel. Deep into the Amazonian jungle, on a moonshine boat, where swarms of insects tormented her sleepless nights with fevered visions of her prior loveless relationship with Alex and his "pets." Disney World during a spring break, where one had to stand in line for hours with over excited brats and their cranky parents. Only to finally discover that Virgil, still the love her life at the time, had returned to the political war front in Oklahoma, and was waging a fierce fight to the death against climate change Deniers! She rushed to his side to join the Cause of course, but he'd been strangely stand-offish, no doubt fearful of putting her at risk. And sure enough...

A pickup truck came to a skidding halt in a patch of poultry litter that served as the house trailer's front yard. A man wearing a gray hoodie got out of the vehicle. Charlene took aim with the shotgun and pulled the trigger.

Click.

Damnit, she'd neglected to insert fresh shells after firing the double-barreled weapon earlier that morning at what proved to be a Tom turkey on the prowl. Frantically, she reloaded...

"Honey, I'm home."

For cryin' out loud, the intruder was Virgil himself, a/k/a "Jake Cooper," not the Mafia hit man from whom they had been hiding for almost two years.

"The van broke down, so I had to cancel my sales calls," he said, after coming into the trailer, taking off his plastic glasses-nose-mustache disguise, then putting a brown paper sack on the kitchenette table. "Borrowed Tom Tom's truck and brought a snack. It's Valentine's Day, ya know, and Tom Tom came up with somethin' special for the occasion: A 'Bleeding Heartburger'."

Charlene gagged. As a somewhat staunch vegetarian—not to mention seven-hundred ninety-four and a half days of sweeping out filthy coops, plus endless nights boiling, plucking and stuffing poultry—she was sick to death of the Tom Tom Diner's menu based entirely on thick slices of "turducken": A nauseating abomination concocted by cramming a dead chicken inside a dead duck inside a dead turkey. The ranch sold smoked whole turduckens worldwide by mail order. "Bone appetito," said Virgil, extending to her a foul sandwich. "There's a surprise stuck in the center, just for you from your one and only."

She turned away in disgust, guzzled the remainder of her "fermented snack," and again gazed through the dirty window into the past. In connection with a mass action lawsuit by Oklahoma farmers and ranchers against big city fossil fuel producers and users, Virgil had become famous again as of two years ago, this time for his traveling demonstrations of the devastating effects of global warming. He was to be the Cause's star witness at the trial. To rightfully share in his triumph, she had forcibly insisted on standing beside him in court, blissfully unaware how far the Oklahoma City oil-and-tar cartel was prepared to go in its diabolical plot to destroy the planet.

Charlene now shivered to recall the sight of the cloaked, unshaven man that intercepted them inside the courthouse, who turned out to be not a humble cleric, there to officiate, say, a wedding. The arch villain, a Fra Guido she later learned, had been hired by OKC's notorious CO2 Gang to "make Virgil permanently disappear." In the process of undertaking that deadly deed, the Fra tied them together with a rope and hauled her away in a gunny sack along with his targeted victim! Eventually, Virgil and she managed to escape the swarthy would be assassin's clutches, and since then had assumed fake identities of an ordinary married couple: "Jake and Jenny Cooper," supposedly undocumented immigrants from—per Virgil's bright idea for getting her hired at the poultry ranch—Turkey.

Without shifting her eyes from the distant northern horizon, Charlene asked: "Anybody in town say anything about an Italian padre passing through, striking up casual conversations in a distinct New Jersey accent?" From over her shoulder, "Nah, I reckon ol' Guido has lost the odor of our Oklahoma scents by now," Virgil replied, as had lately become his annoying mantra. "After all, Sweetie Pie, the big city oil and tar companies came out alright in that legal scuffle with the ranchers and farmers, thanks to..."

No doubt in reaction to her reaching for the rolled-up newspaper, Virgil stopped short of yet again mentioning her deservedly abandoned husband, Alex, who had been called to serve as substitute "star witness" in the "legal scuffle" to save humanity, and failed miserably. "But folks in town are buzzin' about a truckload of Cajuns from Louisiana who came through, on their way to California."

Charlene clenched her hold on the rolled-up "fly swatter," braced herself for what would next come out of Virgil's befowled mouth, and sure enough: "They say that out there in Hollywood you can walk along the road and pick oranges right off a tree."

Charlene swiveled to confront the now raven-haired, now strictly Platonic, now increasingly insignificant "other" for whom she had sacrificed all.

SWAT!

Stunned by the blow to his ear, her erstwhile "Romeo" took the turducken "valentine" from his lips. "Now, now, Honey, I'm just sayin'..."

She was in no mood to listen to his *Grapes of Wrath* sales pitch. With *Everlasting Leadware* now banned from all but one country in the entire world, and Virgil unwilling to relocate to North Korea, he had struggled to find other means of practicing his art of door-to-door sales. Currently, his stock-and-trade was used tires. Not re-treads, but to the contrary: Old tires scraped clean of any remaining "sources of friction" whatsoever, that he hawked as *Easy Rider Road Rubbers*, "guaranteed to completely eliminate friction and increase mileage when properly lubricated with petroleum jelly." People in the area, mainly Mexican agricultural workers, were eager to place orders but generally unable to make even fifty-cent down payments. So Virgil, like a member of the literary Joad family who got left behind the fabled Okie migration to a land of milk and honey—and orange juice—had become unbearably monotonous about how wonderful their life together could and would be in "Hollywood."

On the radio, Paul Simon began to musically list "fifty ways to leave your lover." Virgil took a big bite out of the Bleeding Heartburger. Ignoring the unspoken but crystal clear warning look she gave him, "Maybe I oughta just sneak on out there to check on things," he said, chewing. "Ya know, to make sure the coast is clear, then send back a bus ticket for you when..." Shocked to realize that the former love of her life was obviously plotting to leave her, Charlene put down her fly swatter and reached for the shotgun.

Make a new plan, Stan/ You don't need to be coy, Roy...

After wrapping Virgil's entire body in duct tape, Charlene picked up the wallet she'd taken from his hip pocket. Without much hope of finding more than a couple of bucks...A small slip of paper dropped like a dead moth to the grimy floor. Upon examination, it proved to be a yellowed snippet of newspaper clipping, dated by hand in pencil *10/23* of last year. That was at about the same time Virgil, bedridden with a severe flare-up of hemorrhoids, had become so needy in the face of her hints of leaving him, Charlene recalled, as she read that *Wayne Newton won this year's Nobel Peace Prize...* followed by a heading, ***Past Winners...*** followed by a list of names: *Reverend James "Jimbo" Sharp, Professor Alexander Lehough...* Alex?! Tens of thousands of dollars went along with Nobel Prizes, at least ninety percent of which were rightfully hers!

Hop on the bus, Gus/ You don't need to discuss much...

After packing a few things and putting on a black burka—a gift from Virgil to hide her identity—Charlene paused in the doorway of the dingy house trailer to look back at the messy ending of her romantic folly: At the kitchenette table, a housefly settled onto a clot of bright red juice that had seeped from a pierced cherry embedded in sugary white pulp still partially stuffed into a broken chocolate shell: The bleeding heart, so to speak, of a fallen turducken.

Just drop off the key, Lee/ And get yourself free.

Five

At the *buzz, buzz, buzz, buzz, buzz, buzz* buzzing of her singles-only Shangri-La apartment doorbell, Henrietta jumped out of bed. What in tarnation?! She ran to the door, opened it, and... Wynona Sue brushed past her into the living room. At the sight of Butch "Walter" Bernard asleep on the divan, her mother wheeled around. There was fire in her bloodshot eyes. "Well, now I see why my daughter was too...too busy to take my nine-one-one calls last night," she said. "<u>You</u> were making whoopee when I needed a tourniquet wrapped around my bleeding heart!" Though Butch and she had only got as far as some light sparkin', Henrietta didn't deny the "whoopee" charge. For crying out loud, yesterday was Valentine's Day; she'd had nothing to do and no one to do it with last night. Having spotted Butch in her high school yearbook earlier..."For crying out loud, Henrietta," said her mother, "yesterday was Valentine's Day and...and..." Wynona Sue set down on the front edge of the divan next to Butch's head, took a sheet of tissue paper out of her purse and blew her nose. "Alex, the love of my life," she squeaked, "has brought an 'other woman' into our bed."

Henrietta, shocked to hear of such behavior, set her own self down on the edge of the divan. Her mother moderated herself and commenced to tell her latest tale of heartbreak: "I began to get suspicious night before last," she said. "Alex arrived at the house, not exactly tipsy but already kind of drowsy, even though it was barely six o'clock. So after we'd had a couple of Friendly Creature highballs and...Well, anyway, even though it was our first date, I thought it would be safer for him to, uh, stay over," she said, with a glance toward Butch. "And at sometime in the middle of the night, he began to toss and turn and...Henrietta, Alex actually cried out the other floozie's name, not once, not twice..."

Both relieved and annoyed, Henrietta got up from the divan and went into the kitchenette to make coffee. Wynona Sue followed her. "I know what you're thinking," her mother said; "that Alex was calling out for 'Charlene', his ex so-called 'better half,' who left him for Virgil, of all people. Alex should have stoned her for adultery, and Virgil too, but turned over his other cheek. He's a lover, not a stoner." Henrietta offered her mother a cold biscuit, but she kept on ranting. "Oh yes, Alex is a lover; no doubt he's had many affairs of the heart since forgiving and forgetting that brazen ex-wife; including that snooty socialite in Oklahoma City, Bobbi Kaye Something, for one, his square dance partner at that charity ball for ticks. Her tits were obviously fake, they didn't even move during the lively promenades home, and Alex testified against her and her oil-rich husband in that trial you wrote about for *The New York Times*. No, it was not that brazen bleach-blonde hussy, 'Boobi' Kaye, he was tossing and turning and... dreaming about." Wynona Sue finally paused to catch her breath, and reload her bladder of gall.

"And then, last night…It was Valentine's Day, for crying out loud!"

With the aid of two more tissues, her mother went on to tell about lighting musk candles in every room of her little house on Trudgeon Street, putting a bottle of sparkling white wine in the ice box, and of course dabbing perfume here and there, only to have Professor Lehough show up and "do it to her again"— fall asleep, toss, turn, and cry out the name of "that…that Jezebel!"

"Jezebel?"

"Her name is Zander."

"Zander?"

"Possibly 'Sandy'. I have wracked my brain all night and come up with only…I can't believe it could be Sandra Johnson. She's gotten to be, well, it would take a big loop to rope her, and she's now back to dishwater blonde, not the brunette type who could be a…a homewrecker."

Henrietta sympathized with Wynona Sue for going so quick from smitten to mitten. On the other hand, due to lots of prior experiences with two-timing men, her mother was inclined to be overly…

"I'm not the kind of woman to be unsecure, suspicious and jealous," she claimed. "But I know what 'other' women are capable of when it comes to catching a man like Alex."

"Well, like they say: There are lots of fish in the sea. I reckon another fella just like the professor will soon come along."

"Not for me, Henrietta. Alex Lehough is the love of my life. An 'other' desperate, man-crazy Jezebel will hook him over my dead body."

Butch Bernard came into the kitchenette, wearing only his undershorts, rubbing sleep from his eyes. Though he'd drunk only one slightly spiked glass of water last night at the P's-n-Q's,

Henrietta had made her own self a designated driver, brought him home to her place, and now he looked as hung over as Wynona Sue. She introduced them to one another and..."Holy smokes, girls," Butch said, "did we have one of those French menage de troughs on the divan last night? Yuk, yuk, yuk."

Yeah, he was a dork. But at the muddy bottom of the small pond she lived in, Henrietta had discovered that "Walter-Call-Me-Butch" Bernard seemed to be on his way to becoming a big catfish of sorts. And he was likable enough for occasional company, as well as smarter than an acre of garlic...about some things, not yet including sparkin'.

Six

Max Morgan sat in a semi-enclosed cubicle inside the new Mr. Quickie's copy store on Main Street, refreshing his grasp of an instructional manual of sorts. He had first read *I, The Jury* thirty years ago, upon discovery of the classic Mickey Spillane private detective novel in his deceased father's attic cache of adult literature. Aroused by the naughty vibe of the paperback book's cover—a garish colored ink depiction of a sexy blonde half-wearing an unbuttoned off-white blouse, staring into the muzzle of a handheld gun in the foreground—he had followed the hardboiled hero of the story, Mike Hammer, to an exciting, uh, climax on the lurid tale's final page: *Beautiful as you are, as much as I almost loved you...* Max now again vividly pictured Spillane's account of the blonde "hooking her thumbs in the fragile silk of her panties and pulling them down...walking toward him with outstretched arms...licking her lips...sighing...leaning forward to kiss him..." At age thirteen, he was forever hooked on so-called pulp fiction private eye cases.

Born flat-footed, his body still almost hairless, and pear-shaped even back then, he'd had neither aptitude nor interest in physical activities. Reading and fantasizing about crime detection became his passionate pastime. *My Gun Is Quick... Vengeance Is Mine...One Lonely Night...Girl Hunters...The Big Kill*...Max vicariously experienced, over and over again, all of Mike Hammer's pursuits of personal justice in a tawdry world of violence and s-e-x. Later, he got into Raymond Chandler's not quite so erotically raw adventures of another private hawkshaw, Phillip Marlowe, in *The Big Sleep...Farewell, My Lovely...The High Window...Lady In the Lake...Little Sister...The Simple Art of Murder.* Other heroes in other favorite cases included Rex Stout in *Over My Dead Body* and *The Final Deduction*, Lew Archer in *The Moving Target*, William Crane in *The Dead Don't Care* and of course Max Latin in the *Dime Detective Magazine* story titled *Don't Give Your Right Name*, to name only a few.

Though the *Mike Hammer* TV series had just ended, throughout his teenaged years he also studied the famous shamus, Sam Spade, in countless TV re-runs of *The Maltese Falcon* movie starring Humphrey Bogart as Sam, and watched numerous other similar black-and-white "noir" films, as well as contemporary TV detective series: *Remington Steele...Ace Crawford, Private Eye...Spenser for Hire...Magnum P.I.* and the like. But while it had become hard enough by then for Max to still personally identify with hardboiled dick, Mike Hammer, even moreso Phillip Marlowe—described in print as "six feet of iron, one-hundred and ninety pounds"—for him to actually see himself as, say, a handsome P.I. portrayed by actors such as Pierce Brosnan and Tom Selleck was beyond his waning ability to suspend disbelief. His mother advised him to think of himself as Jessica Fletcher and work exclusively on *Murder, She Wrote* cases.

Max shifted his massive buttocks in the undersized chair provided by Mr. Quickie and let out a mournful sigh. After graduating high school and starting work as a mail carrier, he'd put aside childish things—a prize yo-yo with his name etched on it by a Filipino champion, a tuba, private eye pulp files, his fantasies—but only grudgingly. In the course of making his daily deliveries he'd developed a kind of hobby of noticing and sometimes reporting things not on the up-and-up: A local tomcat, so to speak, sneaking out of a married Mrs. So-and-So's back door. A certain regular recipient of disability insurance checks, lifting an anvil in her driveway. Fairly often, he would spot a tag number listed in the *Police Log* section of the *Weekly Herald* for a "bent iron," detective jargon for stolen car. Later in his career, following his promotion to sorting mail at the post office, he had made a practice of sniffing colored envelopes from and to dames, especially around the time of Valentine's Day; sneaking peeks into packages suspiciously wrapped in plain brown paper; noting return addresses of mail marked *FINAL NOTICE* ; and again fairly often, responding to requests from cops, lawyers and bill collectors for forwarding addresses of persons gone missing. So, to a degree, he had kept his hopelessly fallen arches in the gumshoe game, until his retirement three years ago.

Recalling the boredom that followed—living twenty-four hours a day with his long-widowed mother in the house where he'd grown-up; snacking his only hobby—Max again sighed. If he had not gone online in desperate search of a miracle, he would now tilt the scales at over three-hundred pounds, without physical ability to get out of bed each morning for breakfast. Googling for a fat man help site, he had discovered—Praise the Lord—that back in the mid-1940s noted author, Dashiell Hammett himself, creator of Sam Spade and Nick Charles a/k/a "The Thin Man," had also brought to life on radio a third private detective, and promising new heroic role model. Thank God, a few episodes of the oldtime series were available on CD. Recalling now the excitement of inserting the first disc into his computer, Max's pulse quickened.

First came the sound of heavy footsteps: *Clomp, clomp, clomp.* Then a woman's sultry voice: *There he goes…into that drugstore… he's stepping on the scale.* Then the *kerplunk* of a coin dropping into a slot, followed by the sultry voice again: *Weight: Two-hundred forty-three pounds…*

Sound effect of a card ejecting from a slot like a dollar bill from an old fashioned ATM. *Fortune: Danger!* said the dame's voice, followed by a dramatic musical chord. *Whoooo is it?*

And in a man's low, rumbling, sophisticated baritone drawl: *The Fat Mannnnn.*

At long last, a heavyweight hero he could fully identify with, Brad Runyon: Middle-aged, but still hip to the scene. Overweight, but light on his feet and a good dancer. Hardboiled, but also refined and a dapper dresser. Smart and unflappable when confronted with dangerous twists and turns in cases of murrr-derrrr. Max's suspension of disbelief in Brad Runyon, and himself, was instantaneous and, he resolved, permanent.

In a matter of weeks, he completed fifty hours of vo-tech instruction and submitted an application for an Unarmed P.I. License. Unable to grow a Brad Runyon mustache, but confident of passing an upcoming exam, he had otherwise fully equipped himself to make his lifetime dreams come true. In a vintage clothes store in Tulsa, he found a black-banded gray fedora, pinstriped double-breasted suit, clip-on bow tie and a slightly used pair of two-tone—brown-and-white—wing-tip shoes, all similar to what Brad Runyon wore. At an Army-

Navy surplus store in Okmulgee, he bought a shoulder-holstered plastic replica of a .45 caliber semi-automatic gat that looked just like Mike Hammer's "old junior," plus a set of handcuffs a/k/a "bracelets." From Mr. Quickie right there in town, he ordered a supply of business cards, a printed desk plaque, and bargained for permission to use the in-store paperwork cubicle as his office in return for providing Notary Public services to copy shop customers. From inside his own head came a catchy moniker—"Maximo."

So now, there he sat, sharpening the hardboiled mindset and street lingo required of a private eye. For the umpteenth time, Maximo heard the roar of the .45 shake the room, saw the Mickey Spillane blonde bombshell "stagger back a step... her eyes an unbelieving witness to truth. . . slowly looking down at the ugly swelling in her naked belly where the bullet went in... seeing a thin trickle of blood..." In the hardboiled person of Mike Hammer, he himself turned his head to look at a rubber plant behind him and...

"Could you please help me?" said a woman's voice from across Max's desk. He fully swiveled and saw...Not just an ordinary dame, a real dish: strawberry blonde, eyes like luscious ripe blueberries floating in a bowl of creamy white face. Ordinarily, he was a ham-and-eggs kind of guy, but there was something about this broad that made his mouth water. "I need you to stamp these," she said, dropping two sheets of paper on the desk, then dropping herself into a chair across from him and beginning to put her Jane Hancock on the documents. As Max proceeded to notarize the skirt's signatures, "Hmmm? 'Private Investigations'," she said, in a hesitant tone, reading aloud the desk plaque. "Discretion Guaranteed'. Hmmm ?"

Maximo leaned back in his chair. In a voice as deep as he

could muster, "Mannn trouble?" he drawled.

"What? What on earth are you talking about?" she said, flustered. "I'll have you know, uh, Mister Maximo, I am in love with a wonderful, caring, faithful, trustworthy...How much do you charge for a discreet, <u>very</u> discreet, private investigation?"

Flustered himself to have doped out a case so easily, Maximo played for time by sniffing the plastic red carnation stuck to the wide lapel of his double-breasted suit, while sneaking a peek at the babe's signature: *Wynona Sue Hebert.* "For you, Honey, no charrrge. Sing to me."

Hers was the same old sob song every private dick from Henryetta to Hoboken had heard a thousand times before: She's single, lives by herself, obviously lonely and vulnerable. A guy, name of Alex Lee Ho, comes sniffin' around the honey pot, feeds her a line, and the next thing she knows, the joker is the love of her life. Church bells begin to jingle inside her head. She starts shopping online for a wedding dress. But like every other smooth talking schmo who was ever the love of the Jane's life, this Dick also turns out to have a wandering eyyye. And even though lover boy has as much as confessed to having a little something on the siiide, she can't, or won't believe the awful truth. She wants a discreet private in-ves-ti-gaaation "only to prove there is nothing to 'Alex's' relationship" with a little number known to her only as "Zannn-derrr." Hmmm? Maximo mentally rolled local names and addresses from a handy memorized rolodex, but came up craps. Hmmm? "'Zander' could be your Mr. Hooo's Asian pet name for the other bim-boooo."

"Pet name?" His client struck a hand-to-chin thoughtful pose. "Why yes," she said, "it could be that this...this 'Zander'... is a hissing cockroach from the Madagascar region of Asia."

Hissing cockroach? For all his hardboiled reading, Max never failed to be shocked by how bitterly vindictive a wronged dame could be. "Jumping to concluuusions could be dangerous, Ms. Hebert. I suggest you put this case in my professsional hands before a cat fight breaks out and leads to...murrr-derrr."

"Yes, you're right," she said. "I need to be certain of 'Zander's' identity and, uh, any sordid particulars of her relationship with my fiance before, uh, exterminating the little pest."

After straightening out a couple of incidental details—a Professor L-e-h-o-u-g-h was not a Chinaman for instance—Ms. Hebert a/k/a Wynona Sue ankled out of Max's cubicle. Hmmm? "Zander?" The name rang a bell, but...Given that his client was a strawberry blonde, he had a hunch the "other woman" was sure to be a bruuunette. Yeah, for a lotta guys, different foods for different moods were the spice of life. He himself never had calves liver on consecutive days. Hmmm? "The Face" came to mind. That's what they called the dark haired dame who showed up in every second generation *Mike Hammer* TV re-run, for just a few fleeting moments. The vamp never said a worrrd, played cat-and-mouse, always gave Mike the come on—a smile, a wink, a blown kissss—then took a fade, gave him the dodge, sometimes putting on a vanishing act that not even Mandrake the Magician could pull off. He, Max, still regularly watched the clips of her appearances on *YouuuTuuube*, set to music. And the guy who posted words from a song in the site's comment box had the babe's mystique figured to a teeee. "With that face/ It's not the kill/ It's the thrill...of the chase." Tonight, he would enter the murky noir, stake out the two-timing fiance's digs and put the peep on the mysterious other woman known only by the possibly Dutch, or Polish, or some other foreign pet name, "Zannn-derrr." In the meantime, back to studying for the P.I. exam:

I stood up in front of her and shoved the gun into my pocket... As always when reading the final page of *I, The Jury*, Max was appalled that the blonde seductress who Mike was almost in love with had planted her own rod behind a rubber plant, with the safety catch off and a silencer attached. Yeah, just as Spillane astutely observed, "her loving arms would have reached it nicely. The face that was waiting to be kissed was really waiting to be splattered with blood when she blew Mike's head off."

How c-could you? she gasped.

Mike, and indirectly Maximo, had only a moment before talking to a corpse, but as always, they got it in: *It was easy.*

Seven

By the time she got to work about an hour late, Henrietta's mind was re-set. After telling her boss, Mr. Harold Mixon, about her recent date with Butch, she announced she was going to drop out of online college. "Oh my, don't make that mistake, Henrietta," said Mr. Harold, who had sorta become one of those father figures to her. "Gals who give up on their own ambitions 'cause of infatuation with a boyfriend never fail to regret it." Butch Bernard was not a boyfriend of hers and likely never would be, she protested. "But like I said, even though Butch never even finished high school he knows useful things about almost everything. He makes robots in his mama's garage, advertises 'em online as *Mechanical Soul Mates* and sends 'em off to places all over the world, mainly Japan. To tell the truth, Mr. Harold, studying up on such matters as classic love stories in old books seems to me useless as back pockets on a shirt."

A liberal arts education would enrich her life in ways she could not now foresee, for the very reason that she presently lacked one, said Mr. Harold, who had gone off to Princeton University in his youth and majored in Religion, but came back to his little ol' hometown to take over the *Weekly Herald* from his daddy. "As much or more than science and technology, study of literature, history and art will help you understand what goes on in the world around you, and inside you. And besides, you've already paid tuition, Henrietta," he said, heading for the door, likely to attend an Odd Fellas Lodge buffet brunch up in Okmulgee. "Your mind would also be a terrible thing to waste. Food for thought, Henrietta, food for thought."

After chewing on "food for thought" off and on through the morning, Henrietta realized she was almost scared to further "examine the mystery of literature's same old story of passion, jealousy and hate." Yesterday's lecture—forcing her to face up to the fact that Gaylord and her were never meant for each other—had been hurtful. On the other hand, Butch, who obviously knew A-to-Z about scientific things, had seemed real interested in her telling him she was enrolled in a college English Department course about "the classic love story." And at her singles-only Shangri-La apartment later, when they were semi-sparking on the living room divan, he'd said, "Golly, Henrietta, if you brought your old school books over to Mama's garage sometime, maybe we could work together on a project that's got me stumped."

Hmmm? Though still doubtful about enriching her life, but ashamed of herself for being a fraidy cat, Henrietta pulled up her socks and went back to class:

Professor LeRoy:

With the afterglow of Valentine's Day now faded, I trust it is safe for me to disabuse some of you of any notion you may have about "Cupid," as portrayed by Hallmark Cards. Cupid is the name ancient Romans used for the Greek god Eros—mischievous son of Aphrodite,

Goddess of Love—and represents a force within humankind not necessarily having much to do with Valentine's Day sentimentality. Today, we shall address a classic love story that first appeared almost two thousand years ago in a book titled Metamorphoses—the ageless story of Psyche and Eros, to-wit:

Psyche was the most beautiful woman ever born, but cold, asexual, unapproachable, without prospects of marriage. Her concerned father went to see an oracle, who advised that there was no future for Psyche except to wed a horrible monster with power to destroy the world. Meanwhile, the Goddess Aphrodite had become increasingly jealous of Psyche's beauty that many said surpassed her own divine good looks. In a rage, and given that her power was to mischiefly cause mortals and gods to fall in love, she instructed her naughty boy, Eros, to tip his arrows with a love potion and prick Psyche at the moment she first laid eyes on a monster, dooming her to a life of marital misery. Eros dutifully flew to Psyche's lonely bed chamber, saw her in semi-darkness, sleeping, and guess what? He accidentally pricked himself with one of his arrows, instantly fell in love with Psyche, and took her to live in his wondrous castle.

Charlie Morrison:

And "pricked" her there in his crash pad, I'll bet.

Professor LeRoy:

Not with one of his arrows, no, but he did come to her every night, always in darkness, and—after she promised to never look upon his face—introduced Psyche to wild, passionate, ecstatic sex.

Barbara Jean Booker:

What bullshit! A typical male fantasy of wild, passionate, ecstatic date rape.

Agnetta Hurley:

Trigger! Trigger! Trigger! Somebody call Dean Rottweiler!

Professor LeRoy:

An astute observation on your part, Ms. Booker. Though I understand many feminists now relate favorably to Psyche and Eros as a woman's story, I disagree. Just as "Cupid" is the Roman name for the Greek god Eros, the Roman term for the Greek mortal Psyche—meaning Soul—translates literally as "Anima," about which we will hear more later in the course. In the works of Carl Jung, and perhaps from my own novel, titled "The Same Old Story" (available through Amazon for $ 9.99). You see, the cultures of ancient Greece and Rome were patriarchal, the philosophical storytellers were men, and like most if not all of their myths, the story of Psyche and Eros is metaphor for a male's psychological struggles and development, which I hope you will see as my summary progresses, to-wit:

Jealous of Psyche's happiness, her two sisters—who in fairness to them, had heard the oracle's prophecy—convinced her that she was sleeping with a monster who had power to destroy the world and would kill her—along with them—if she did not kill him first. And so, when Eros fell asleep after hours of intense love making, Psyche lit a candle, grabbed a knife, and guess what? As she looked upon Eros for the first time and saw how beautiful he was, she accidentally pricked herself on the sharp tip of one of his arrows that he had left in a quiver hung on a bed post. Psyche fell in love with Eros.

Barbara Jean Booker:

And they lived happily ever after until the love potion wore off, which usually takes about eighteen months.

Agnetta Hurley:

Sometimes eighteen minutes.

Professor LeRoy:

Indeed, in the words of the Bard: "The course of love never runs smooth." A drop of hot wax from the candle fell upon Eros' shoulder. He woke with a start, saw that Psyche had broken her promise to not look upon his face, and flew away into darkness. Fortunately, I dare say, we do not have time to go into the steps Psyche had to take to win back Eros. Suffice it to say, in the end the supreme god, Zeus, officially made Psyche divine, she wedded Eros, and together they had a child named Joy.

Barbara Jean Booker:

Oh goody, a "happy ending" in marriage and a kid. Followed by the sequel a few years later, Splitsville, featuring "dramatic" arguments in divorce court about who had to pay for Joy's braces.

Professor LeRoy:

Quite so in many real life love stories. In literature, marriage is metaphor. Per one of many aphorisms penned by Oscar Wilde—who by the way, was gay, not that there is anything whatsoever wrong with that—to-wit: "All tragedies end in death/ All comedies end in marriage" (lol).

Barbara Jean Booker:

Same sex marriage is not a joke, Professor LeRoy. SAME SEX MARRIAGE IS NOT FUNNY!

Agnetta Hurley:

BAN STRAIGHT SEX! BAN STRAIGHT SEX FOR GUYS!

Professor LeRoy:

As I say, in literature "marriage" is metaphor, for Man's <u>*and*</u> *Woman's achievement of the sublime wholeness they sense having once had, but lost. It's the quintessential happy ending, if you will, of comedy, which is a literary term for a narrative not ending in death.*

Barbara Jean Booker:

DEATH TO LITERARY HATE SPEECH! DEATH TO UNFUNNY COMEDY!

Agnetta Hurley:

COLLEGE IS A SAFE SPACE! MAKE PROFESSOR

LEROY LEAVE US ALONE!CALL DEAN ROTTWEILER!

Barbara Jean Booker:

DEATH TO HOMOPHOBIC REPUBLICANS! DEATH TO PROFESSOR LEROY!

Land sakes alive! Henrietta feared her classmates were about to stir up a riot, and... Uh-oh, now nameless others had gathered like flies on a spilt sno-cone and started shouting slogans such as had been hollered by outsiders on Main Street during the last Mayoral election.

BLACK LIVES MATTER! BLACK LIVES MATTER MORE! ONLY BLACK LIVES MATTER!

STAND UP FOR TRANSGENDER URINATION RIGHTS!

PUT CHE'S FACE ON THE YANQUI DOLLAR!

DIVEST U.S. BONDS!

GUNS KILL! BAN GUNS!

WORDS HURT! BAN WORDS!

WIPE OUT WHITENESS!

WE WANT DIVERSITY!

LET MY PEOPLE PEE!

Henrietta was thankful the class was only online and the uproar only virtual. If poor Professor LeRoy had been on a real-life campus, there was no telling what harm might have come to him.

CANCEL STUDENT DEBT!

NO MORE TUITION!

FAIR WAGES FOR STUDENTS!

NO MORE HOMEWORK!

NO MORE CLASSES!

NO MORE COLLEGES!

Charlie Morrison:

PANTY RAID AT THE THETA HOUSE! BE AT RILEY'S BAR BY EIGHT TONIGHT!

Dean Rottweiler:

STOP IT! *AND I MEAN. .* ***NOW!***
ALL OUTSIDE "KIBITZERS". . . ***OUT!***
ALL REGISTERED STUDENTS . . . ***SUSPENDED!***
ALL TRAUMA COUNSELING. . . ***CANCELED!***

Barbara Jean Booker:

We're sorry, Dean Rottweiler.

Agnetta Hurley:

We didn't mean nothing by what we said.

Dean Rottweiler:

AND ANYONE WHO ATTEMPTS TO TAKE PANTIES FROM ANYWHERE ON CAMPUS FOR WHATEVER REASON WILL BE ***DE-PANTS*** *IN THE QUAD, SPANKED, AND SENT HOME TO MAMA WITH ROSY CHEEKS!* ***UNDERSTOOD?***

Charlie Morrison:

We were just funnin', Dean Rottweiler. Honest.

The screen went blank. . .and stayed blank, leaving Henrietta to feel like a goat staring at a new gate, no more able to understand anything about the world around and inside her than before she signed up for a liberal arts college education.

Eight

Again at his bathroom lavatory, Alex once more groomed for a night of sheer bliss, sleeping with Wynona Sue in a veritable Garden of Eden. *Take me with you, Alex*, said Zander from within him. *I promise not to whisper anything in your ear at an, uh, inopportune moment that would spoil the mood.* Alex was dubious. Throughout the past few days, his "other self" had become increasingly jealous of his relationship with Wynona Sue, the fantastic woman he'd fallen head-over-heels in love *and lust* with. *I simply referred to her as seeming somewhat more like the first wife, less an "Eve" than a "Lilith," so to speak: A veritable succubus who seduces you in your sleep and sends you home the next morning feeling spent.* "That's after-glow," Alex mumbled, "and I deserve a hot time after all these years, living alone with no one to..." *Thanks a lot, Alex. I thought we were blissfully happy together since the wife ran off with Virgil Carter.* Dog gone it, why did Zander always bring up Charlene and try to ruin his mood for what Wynona Sue—in her genteel, ladylike way—called "whoopee"?

Alex reached into the medicine chest above the lavatory for

the brown bottle of powerful potion that would put the nagging pest to sleep, but...

CRASH!

A large black bird of some kind flew through a window into the bathroom! *It's her! The cockatrice! The two-legged, winged reptile herself!* The black-clad figure—somewhat resembling a giant hissing cockroach—stood to a height of more than five feet. It then removed the Darth Vader-like vented cloth helmet of a burka to reveal a spiked, platinum blonde *head of a chicken! It's her alright, Alex, the cockatrice!*

"Long time, no see, Alex," said, of all people...

"Charlene... what a surprise... You've... you've... you've... changed your hair."

"A woman's prerogative," she replied, "among numerous others. What's that hissing sound?" She seemed jumpy as a nervous flea.*The cockroaches are excited, Alex. They mistake her for their queen, come to break-off their "tendrils" during acts of "whoopee," then eat what's left of her lovers.*

"A gas leak, just a harmless gas leak," Alex explained. "Let's go into the living room, sit by the fire and..."

"No, let's get re-acquainted in my room. I'm famished."

In the kitchen, "Where is my flyswatter, Alex?" Charlene immediately said. "I left it right here, hanging on this nail." *Watch out, Alex, she's rolling up a newspaper.*

SWAT!

"Have you had the heartless gall to allow your lover, 'Robert K. What's-His-Name', to use, and misplace my things while I was away?" his ex-wife of two years asked. "That is unforgivable of you." *She has a mistaken impression of that big-bosomed Oklahoma City socialite, Bobbi Kaye Boone. She thinks you're gay, but let it slide. Don't risk starting a cat fight between...*

"My do-si-do with Mrs. Bobbi Kaye was just that, a passing fancy. She is a passionate woman who...I am not gay, Charlene, not that there would be anything wrong about that."

"Yeah, sure," said his ex-wife, also a woman *of sorts*. "What about that buddy you used to always mumble about, 'Zander'?"

I'm not gay!

"Zander and I are...we're just friends," Alex explained. "There's nothing romantic about our...our relationship."

"Yeah, that's what all cheaters say," said Charlene, before moving toward the fridge and opening its door. "On the other hand," she said after a thoughtful pause, "some home-wrecking woman has obviously been looking after you, I see." *She's talking about the home cooking you brought back from your date last night. And by the way, why did the fried chicken with all the fixin's go uneaten, Alex? Too busy making 'whoopee'?*

"A Miss Wynona Sue is my lover, I am proud to say," said Alex, proudly. "She too is a passionate woman who..."

"Wynona Sue? You are banging that hairdressing harlot who threw herself at Virgil and then spitefully didn't even vote for him?! That makes your hanky-panky even more unforgivable, Alex, you womanizing bastard! In fact...What's was that sound? Is somebody here?"

Uh oh.

With terror in her eyes, a chicken leg in one raised hand and the rolled-up newspaper in the other, Charlene swiveled her spiked head toward a kitchen window, then in the direction the bedroom they had once *or twice* shared. "Is little Miss Wynona Sue here? Have you brought your harlot into our happy home? If so, Alex, I have every right to scratch her eyes out, and I will!"

SWAT!

As his ex-wife stormed toward the bedroom, Alex retreated

to the bathroom and called Wynona Sue on his cell phone. "Where are you, Alex?" she said. "It's already almost seven and I have a surprise...Oh well, guess what I've planned for dinner tonight? Zander!"

See, Alex, if you will only keep your pants on, the three of us can get along, enjoy ourselves just dining together and chatting, like friends.

"I happened to be looking through a...a cookbook, and discovered that a Zander is a fish! So I had a frozen one flown in from Dallas. But if you don't hurry, well, I had planned for us to skip highballs, perhaps for a quickie, and afterward pick the Zander bones clean."

"Honey, I'm sorry, but something has come up and..."

"Why are you whispering, Sweetie? I can barely hear your voice."

"ALEX! GET YOUR ASS IN HERE! WE NEED TO TALK!"

"Is someone there?"

"No, no one...Yes, a plumber, to fix a gas leak. So I won't be able to make whoopee tonight, Honey. Things could blow up over here at any second. Gotta go."

In the living room, Charlene sat in a chair beside a flameless fireplace, rolled-up newspaper still in hand. "Alex, I've tried, lord knows how I have tried to save our marriage despite your repeated AC/DC philandering," she said with a sigh, "but I just can't do it anymore. I want a divorce."

"A divorce? But...but...but..." *I told you, Alex: As writ on the outhouse wall: "The job's not done 'til the paperwork is done." She's still your legal spouse, come back to pick your bones clean. Give her twenty pounds of flesh and get rid of her, permanently.* "But Charlene, you ran off with Virgil Carter two years ago, and even before that..."

"Virgil and I were just friends. We shared only a deep

commitment to bankrupting the oil and gas industry in order to…And by the way, what did you say at that trial to set back our propaganda war against carbon emissions? For cryin' out loud, Albert Schweitzer and Mother Teresa? Okay. The Dalai Lama and Yassir Arafat? Sure. Al Gore and Barrack Obama? Slam dunks. Wayne Newton? Eh. But you, Alexander Lehough?"

Aha, the harpy has flown out of the "Woods of Self-Murderers" in Dante's seventh ring of hell, taken a break from tormenting victims of suicide, to get her claws on the, heh heh, "Nobel Prize" money! Give her a twenty, Alex, tell her to keep the change and go back! go back! go back into the woods!

Alex cleared his throat. "Well, Charlene, now that you ask: Though only a luke warmist at best regarding the so-called science pointing to CO2 emissions as the cause of climate change, I nevertheless testified for our state's farmers and ranchers seeking monetary damages to achieve restoration of cattle and deer herds, but more importantly, to save the dependent tick population. In that context and courtroom venue, I was given the opportunity to introduce to the scientific and political communities, as well as to the public at large, my Lone Star Tick and Alfa Gal Theory."

Zzzzzzzzzzzzzzzzzzzzzzzzzzzzz…

"You wouldn't happen to have a quart-size bottle of aspirin handy, would you?" Charlene asked. She was a scientist of only the social type and had always been susceptible to sudden onset of headaches during their interesting conversations about what really mattered, Alex recalled. But no, the only remedy he had on hand was the potent potion reserved for Zander.

"You see, a variety of tick native to Texas—The Lone Star Tick—has a unique relationship with alfa-gal, which of course is a sugar carbohydrate. He's a carrier from non-primate mammals, and when he transmits alfa-gal mixed with tick saliva by bite to humans, we get very sick. One effect is a severe allergy to meat consumption. Given that farts and belches from herds of cattle, along with agricultural manure, emit vast quantities of methane gas into the atmosphere, well, there you have it: Universal vegetarianism would do as much or more for mankind as would going on a fossil-free diet. My testimony backfired on the ranchers—they would have to go out of business—but in the long run..."

"I'm sure your current squeeze—Wynona Sue— finds this kind of chit-chat spell binding," Charlene conceded. "And if you've not done so already, during your next roll in the hay be sure to enthrall her with fascinating facts about the anuses of fireflies. The little whore deserves you. Now, let's get down to the business of divvying up..."

CLOMP! CLOMP! CLOMP!

"Turn off the lights!" Charlene commanded. "Cover me, Alex," she said, obviously terrified. "I'm going to make a run for it!"

What's going on? Is she gone? Did you agree to pay her off?

Through the darkness, Alex heard from the direction of the bathroom the sound of loud frantic hissing, followed by Charlene's voice, shrieking "My lawyer will be in touch!" Then, outside a living room window...the *CLOMP! CLOMP! Clomp! Clomp! clomp!* of hurried heavy footsteps receding into the night.

Whoooo was that? He or she must weigh at least two-hundred and, say, forty-odd pounds, and have hopelessly flat feet.

Nine

At the P's-n-'Q's pool hall and quaint cafe, Henrietta climbed up on Butch Bernard's back and grabbed hold of his right hand with hers. "Okay, okay, I got it," he finally said. "Angle of that yellow ball's course to that hole down there is exactly sixteen, no fifteen-point-six degrees. Shoot!" Henrietta climbed off. Butch was a good analyzer, no doubt, but couldn't seem to get the hang of stroking a pool cue in the right direction. "Why don't we set down and have another glass of water," she suggested; "maybe mix in five or six drops of Who Struck John to calm your nerves some more." Butch, who she had already found to be unordinarily agreeable and eager to learn new things, followed her back their table. After they set down, "Gosh, Henrietta," he said, "where did you learn to play the angles so good, in college?"

She reached across the table, took his eyedropper out of a pocket and dipped it into her glass of straight Who Struck John. "No, I don't have much knowledge of geolometry," she said, reaching across to squeeze a goodly amount of the spiritous liquor into Butch's glass. "I reckon a liberal arts education is what enriches a body's life. So like I said before, I am an English major, studying up on the classic love story in literature." He seemed more impressed than before, maybe some overly so, and asked her to tell him "the classic love story." Though feeling unprepared for a pop quiz..."Well, it all starts in the Bible, back when humans were Siamese twins, some of 'em both male, some both female, and the others one of each. They got uppity, particularly the Adam-and-Eve type, so God came down and cut 'em in two, sewed 'em up, I reckon, and..." She noticed that behind his thick round glasses Butch's eyes had got big and bright—and as rapidly blinking—as those of a devil's face on the screen of a pinball machine behind him.

"I've always been interested in taxidermy," he said, "stuffing squirrels, possums, foxes, a whole horse one time, but...sticking two live humans together to make Siamese twins! That would be somethin'!"

Though worried some about cheating—or rather getting caught at it—Henrietta went on to stuff her report on the classic love story with tidbits of what she already knew about some versions listed in her English course reading list that Professor LeRoy had not yet got to. "All comedies end in marriage," she said, "like *Cinderella* and about every other fairy tale for girls. But all tragedies end in death, like *Romeo and Juliet* that Taylor Swift sang about."

"Golly, Henrietta, you make me wish I had finished high school and enriched myself in college like you."

And a couple of hours later, in the midst of sparking on the divan in her living room, Butch said, "I wish you could teach me the classic love story, Henrietta. So maybe we could work together on that project that's got me stumped."

That sounded semi-interesting to her, but by then there was

another matter he seemed to be having trouble figuring out: A delicate project sorta like shooting pool, the angles of which... Henrietta suddenly realized that Butch, in his early twenties, was awkward 'cause he was a virgin! She rolled him over and climbed on top, but...

KNOCK! KNOCK! KNOCK!

Henrietta got semi-dressed and went to the door. "Now your doorbell don't buzz neither, it seems," said her mother, before barging in again! "You might as well move back home," Wynona Sue said, with nary a glance at Butch there on the divan, now only semi-naked. "As old maids, we can watch television shows together like when you were young, before you met Gaylord." Henrietta handed over a box of tissue paper and braced herself. "I've been jilted, again!" her mother wailed. "I foolishly convinced myself that Alex has been dreaming about...food. I went to a lot of trouble to put on a fish-fry for him and..."

Wynona Sue noticed Butch, shooed him off the divan with a wave of her hand, set down and continued with her latest version of the same old story. "Alex cancelled at the last minute. He called and mumbled something about having gas. But I heard a voice in the background. They're in each other's arms as we speak: Alex and that tramp, Zander!" Her mother paused to blow her nose, then waited to be told she must have mistook what she heard on the phone. Henrietta didn't even try to be a comfort. "I know what you're thinking, Henrietta; that I am being foolish; that I am letting my imagination...Hey, Buster," she shouted at Butch, slinking toward the bathroom. "I need for you to run a little errand."

Her mother explained that because she her own self didn't want to get caught looking unsecure, suspicious and jealous, she wanted Butch to hightail it over to Professor Lehough's house on Division Street, sniff around, and catch him and Zander "in fragrante." Henrietta stomped a foot.

"Professor Lehough?" said Butch. "Heck, he was senior advisor of my Boy Scout troop back in high school. He taught us all about the mating habits of bugs and bees. You don't have to worry none about the professor hangin' out with any female, Ms. Wynona Sue. He had a strict rule: No hetero sex! Yuk, yuk, yuk."

Wynona Sue glared at Butch like he had broke wind or somethin'. "Are you trying to tell me that Zander is a man?!" she hissed. "And Alex one of those gay Boy Scout leaders I keep hearing about?!" She turned from Butch with fear in her eyes. "Oh my God, Henrietta, have I followed you down the primrose path you took with Gaylord Goodhart?"

Henrietta looked over at Butch, standin' there, hiding his "pool cue" behind the skirt she'd left on the divan, grinning like a frog in a feed lot. She wondered, not so much about whether Wynona Sue was on any gay garden path like she'd took with Gaylord, but about whether she her own self had strayed into the footsteps of her desperate mother, and settled for a "Professor Lehough Junior" as a boyfriend.

Ten

From a window seat near the rear of a bus otherwise occupied by persons apparently incapable of speaking English, Charlene gazed through the mesh patch of her black burka into a checkered future possibly even more bleak than her recent past. Following last night's harrowing escape from her former happy home on Division Street, she had found refuge—under the name "Jane Doe"—in a seedy motel on the western edge of downtown Henryetta. Until noon today, she had cowered there, expecting Fra Guido to bust through the door at any moment. Probably the CO2 Gang's relentless henchman had tracked Virgil and her to the Flying Feathers Ranch down in Texas, she imagined. Due to her carelessly soft-hearted farewell gesture for old times' sake—punching air holes in the duct tape wrapped across Virgil's face—the Fra must have found her ex...acquaintance... alive and well. And no doubt the very former love of her life had proved untrue after only minimal torture. Virgil knew Alex had heisted a Nobel Prize and that she would go after her legal husband for her rightful share of the ill-gotten loot.

Men! Charlene belched in disgust, tinged with remorse and burrito. If only Alex had stood by her side until collecting the prize money, she would have started divorce proceedings the very next day. Though the wheels of justice usually ground disfavored husbands into dust at a notoriously slow pace, she could have been free by now, and rich. Alex, ever the wimp, probably would not have even put up a fight. Charlene ground her teeth in frustration. Even as late as last night, she could have physically forced him to hand over her ninety-nine percent piece of the action if the Fra had not come clomping. But now, with the C02 Gang goombah lurking about, she didn't dare go back to the house. No doubt that cheap little gold digger, Wynona Sue, now forewarned, would also be on the lookout for her. And possibly armed. She herself, unarmed and defenseless, needed a white knight to fight on her behalf while she laid low, very low. And time was of the essence. She needed to immediately hire a ball-busting divorce lawyer.

Charlene got off the bus in the county seat town of Okmulgee, about fifteen miles north of Henryetta. On Seventh Street, across from the county courthouse, lawyers' storefront offices were lined up like buzzards on a telephone wire. She peered through the plate glass window of the closest one, entered, and passed through a small, unattended reception area. Sloppily signed in yellow paint on a stained barn wood door: *WILLIS V. WILLIS*, below that, *Country Lawyer*, and next to an open-mouthed alligator decal: *Liti-Gator*.

"Whoa! Whoa! Hold on there!" A mature, heavy-set man stood up behind a cluttered desk with his arms raised. Sweat stains immediately appeared in the armpits of his blue denim work shirt. "I'm not Jewish, Christian, Hinduer or anything else, and I've never been middle-east of anywhere past St. Louis!" It took Charlene fifteen minutes to convince Willis V. Willis she was not a suicide bomber and simply needed a lawyer to get her divorced from a wealthy husband. "Rich, you say," he said, before sitting down at the desk and picking up a pen. "What's the name of the sumbitch who's done you wrong, Mrs....?"

"Lehough, spelled L-e-h-o..."

The jowly lawyer dropped the pen and leaned back in his massive cowhide-upholstered chair. "If you're talkin' about Professor Alexander Lehough, I am conflicted out of the matter," he said. "Your no-good husband consulted me this very morning, sittin' in that very spot you're in."

That sneaky bastard! Charlene was shocked that Alex seemed inclined to be difficult, but..."Drop him and take me," she said. "We might, you know..." she opened the mesh grill of her burka and winked..."have some fun."

"Haven't taken him on, not yet," he said, but then—apparently slow on the uptake—"Sorry, still can't lawyer for you, not now that I have talked to your husband. Might get my own ass sued. That's what 'conflicted out' means."

"There's no conflict. Alex is not a fighter, he's a...not a lover either. He doesn't even need his own lawyer. You could handle it for both of us. I need a quickie."

"Can't do, Mrs. Lehough. And I must advise that both you and your husband do need a lawyer apiece, whether either one of you want one or not. No bar member in the county would represent both of you—or either one against the other who was unlegally represented—for fear of getting his ass sued by the one who later felt screwed, or by both of you. That's ethics, plus liability law. Attorneys around here will sue another lawyer who tries to work both sides of the street quicker than green grass goin' through a goose. We are a litigatin' bunch of sumbitches, includin' yours truly, which is why every man and woman in Okmulgee County can count on gettin' his and her day in court."

Slightly gratified that at least Alex apparently had also been turned down by Willis V. Willis for some reason—she could imagine many—Charlene closed her hinged mesh mask and went next door. Ten minutes later, shit! Alex had window shopped there too; another old buzzard was "conflicted out." And that was the same story she got from lawyers all the way down the street: "Sorry, conflicted out...conflicted out... conflicted out." Obviously there was a male conspiracy afoot to deny justice to wronged women, or just as unconstitutional, to deny expedient mercy to amicable couples such as Alex and her, who were simply sick of each other.

At the end of the block, Charlene herself had sweaty armpits and was all but certain it would not be worth her while to climb a dingy set of stairs to an office above a bail bond store, even though large signs plastered on the upper facade of the two-story brick building seemed to offer exactly what she needed: *THOMAS "SWIFTY" MASHBURN, ATTY...Justice Delayed Is Justice Denied...*and in flashing neon: *GET SWIFTY TO GET 'ER DONE.*

Upstairs, she pushed open a stained-glass inner door. Inside a dimly lit office, the first thing she saw was a large, wall-mounted, brightly illuminated "photograph" of Jesus. A balding, bespectacled, suited-and-vested middle-aged man then came to her from behind a desk in the solemn manner of a kindly parson and extended a soft, warm hand, as though offering funeral condolences to a widow. "Attorney Mashburn, at your service," he said in a quiet tone of voice. Though put off by his gentlemanly manner, she accepted his offer of a chair mainly because she was out of breath from the stair climb. "Swifty" did not have the look of a go-getter. And a large outward facing photo on his desk showed him to be a literally cross-bearing family man, likely to preach to her against divorce. Nevertheless, she stated her business, with emphasis on her urgent need for virtually instant justice. Charlene was almost disappointed when he didn't say he was "conflicted out."

"Sounds like a simple, though sorrowful matter," Attorney Mashburn confirmed from across his tidy desk. "But tell me, Mrs. Lehough, is your husband an adulterer? Has he broken his sacred vows to you, and violated Section Seven of the Ten Commandments Statute? Is he deserving of God's terrible swift sword?"

"Oh yes," she said in answer to the irrelevant question. "Alex has admitted a sexual fling with a Mrs. Bobbi Kaye Somebody. Currently he is banging a little homewrecker named Wynona Sue. There may even be a third 'other woman' in our marital bed, whispering sweet nothings in his ear."

The mild mannered attorney slammed an open palm on his desk and said in an outraged tone, "I'll have that sinful son of a bitch strung up, gutted and skinned by sundown three or four weeks from today."

"Three or four weeks?! I need a quickie, Swifty."

"Five thousand down and I'll get 'er done in ten days, weekend after next."

"Five thousand dollars?! Today? As a down payment?"

"Plus ten percent of the haul on delivery of the carcass. That's standard for emergency service."

"Why is divorce so expensive?"

"Because it's worth it."

Charlene, doubtful that feminine wile would work on the stern "parson," but desperate, opened the hinged mesh veil of the burka and winked. "I'm hot," she said, standing. "Mind if I slip out of this sweat suit?"

"No, no, Mrs. Lehough, I couldn't allow that," the pious parson said, as a beads of sweat appeared between strands of black hair on his balding head. "I'll open a window."

She unzipped the burka halfway down to her waist.

"Well, maybe just a peek," he said, standing, removing his steamed-up wire-rimmed spectacles and commencing to *huff, huff, huff.*

"Nothing down but yours truly," she said. "Flat fee of a grand when justice is delivered on schedule."

"Twenty-five hundred on the barrelhead," he countered, taking off his jacket. *Huff, huff, huff.* "Eight percent of what the professor's worth weighs in at."

"Gimme a break. Four percent straight commission, or I walk the other side of the street."

"Hundred dollar deposit to cover the filing fee." *Huff, huff, huff.* Down went the zipper. *Huff, huff, huff.* Off went the vest. *Huff, huff, huff, huff.* "But I'm firm at six percent."

"Ten bucks right now, right here on the barrelhead. Five percent on the backside."

"Let's get 'er done." *Huff, huff, huff, huff, huff, huff...*

Not much later, carried by cheap public transportation back toward the cheap motel in Henryetta, Charlene again gazed out a window, reflecting on what she had done. In tune with her thoughts, a mournful old country-and-western song titled *Your Cheatin' Heart*—one of Virgil's favorites—wafted from someone's iPhone to the rear of the bus...*Your cheatin' heart/ will pine someday*...she began to feel remorseful...*You'll crave the love/ you threw away*...then consumed with guilt, bereft of all self respect for... *Your cheatin' heart/ will tell on you*...for giving in to Swifty Mashburn. A five percent piece of the action was way more than the money grubbing divorce deacon deserved for handling a quickie divorce!

Eleven

Henrietta braked her yellow Checker to a stop at the curb in front of Professor Lehough's stucco bungalow. She had last seen the professor about two years ago, when the Mayor tried to put on a big golf tournament at the Henryetta Hot Links golf course and town dump out by the hogback hill west of town. One night back then she came upon him setting at a campfire in the dump with a troop of Boy Scouts and Girl Scouts. They regularly got together out there to conduct experiments on dead animals and likely other experiments on each other. A day or two later, to draw attention to older generations taking advantage of the younger one, he led a Scouts protest and read a Mayflies Manifesto on national TV. The golf tournament got cancelled due to a fire on the hogback, likely set by members of the Midlife Crisis Center militia. But when New York bankers tried to foreclose on public golf course bonds, it was Professor Lehough who stopped them. Turned out the dump was home to a rare species of burying beetles as well as mayflies under the protection of the Federal Environmental Agency and the F.B.I.

She liked the professor and had long ago learned to steer clear of her mother's romantic troubles with men. But since running off Butch Bernard a couple of nights ago, Wynona Sue had been on her like stink, nagging at her to do some "investigative reporting" about the professor's sexual preferences in general and for a certain "Zander" in particular. So she had come up with a fake idea for a news story about the approximately same subject of romantic relations in the world of insects, which she knew was where Professor Lehough's heart had been lodged for as long as she had known him. Henrietta felt semi-sneaky about it, but reckoned that sneaky was just a part of the journalism career she had chose back in high school.

Professor Lehough opened his front door, looking his usual disheveled but shorter-haired self, with an also usual confused look on his face. "It's me, Professor," she said, "Henrietta—now spelled with an i—from the newspaper." His eyes lit up, blinking like, well, like fireflies. "Oh, yes," he said. "Has your mother sent me a message. Her phone seems to be out of order, and her doorbell too. I need to tell her something in private, but..."

"That's all between you and Wynona Sue," she said, holding up a "stop" hand signal. "I'm here to do an investigative newspaper story about the love lives of bugs." With eyes even brighter and not blinking, he invited her in and got right to it: "The classic love story of birds, bees and cockroaches goes back to the time of Creation when Mother Nature..." As the professor, as was his habit, went on and on, Henrietta looked around the living room for signs of any recent female company, but saw none. Professor Lehough plopped into an easy chair, opened a picture book and, in that mumbly way of his, kept on talking: "Oh yes, the male cockroach is quite a Romeo," he said. "He postures, emits pheromones—all-natural *Old Spice*, you might say, heh,

heh—he chirps, whistles and some species hiss to attract mates. The 'Juliets' respond in kind of course. They, male and female, dance together in rhythm with their stridulation—that's the acoustic signals they make with their spiracles—and finally, of course, they copulate, often for prolonged blissful periods." The professor looked up from the book, not so bright eyed, and said, "How is your mother, Henrietta? I miss..."

"What about gayness in cockroaches?" she asked, ignoring his question "Do some of the males, uh, choose one of their own for a dance partner?"

"Cockroaches? Well, sometimes it may be not clear who is partnered with whom when the dance floor is crowded and the acoustic beat gets hot and heavy, but as for sexual preference, no; any suggestion that cockroaches are sometimes gay is nothing but politically correct nonsense started in the late 1990s to fit a political agenda. There is a big difference between what might be characterized as 'homosexual behavior'—males cuddling, for instance—and sex. Indeed..." Professor Lehough paused and semi-cocked his head, like he was listening to "stridulations" or somethin' Henrietta couldn't hear. She noticed his left ear was reddish and semi-swelled up. "Right," he said. "Henrietta, I hope you are not going to write anything about cockroach romance that will get it mixed up with the current media folderol about this same-sex marriage fad among humans. Cockroaches are not anything like dragonflies when it gets down to courtin'."

Henrietta was surprised that the professor seemed to disapprove of same-sex marriage. In answer to her question on the subject, he made it clear that in his view—just like that of her boss, Mr. Harold, who was also educated about things—homosexual sex was "contrary to nature." She was semi-relieved to hear that from him, but decided to take another angle at the matter. "According to a certain Boy Scout I happen to know, you advise young fellas to not get involved in hetero sex."

"Oh yes," he admitted, "and Girl Scouts too, of course. It's only natural for young males and females—of all species—when out in the woods, sleeping in tents, listening to the stridulation of others...Well, teenage pregnancies have always been a problem around here, so...I get the feeling your mother might be avoiding me, Henrietta."

For no particular reason, she asked about any passion, jealousy and hate goin' on in the classic love story of birds, bees and cockroaches. Back to brighter out of the eyes, "Oh my, now you've got to the sensational parts of wild romance in nature," he said. "As for birds, one need only observe the mating 'action' of European robins. Indeed, because both male and female are red-breasted and passionate, either will sometimes attack and kill a mate it jealously mistakes for a romantic rival. In the case of cockroaches, we always see a few high status males monopolize mating opportunities by means of various tricks designed to enforce female monogamy, often at the cost of female fitness. Though some say we cannot know their motivations, for they have none, I say look at the supposedly mindless human sperm cell. Most do nothing at all inside a woman, until confronted by another man's sperm, in which case they passionately fight to the death. Whether or not there is actual hate involved, well... Females are not free of blame of course, but...Wynona Sue hasn't taken up with another, has she? Females are wily about mating."

As the professor went back to droning, Henrietta wondered why it was him who was inclined to nod off during dates with Wynona Sue, and not her mother who got put to sleep by his stridulations. Mainly just to cut him off, she asked if she could use the bathroom. "No!" he said in a semi-sharp tone, with a semi-alarmed look in his eyes. "Uh, the little ones are resting and shouldn't be disturbed," he explained. "I was up all night with them, talking about...Please tell Wynona Sue to call me. I have been worried sick about telling her..." Henryetta headed for the front door, opened it, but then recalled another thing on her mind. She turned back to Professor Lehough and found him looking sad as an old beagle dog. "Do you happen to recall a certain Boy Scout, name of Butch Bernard?" she asked. "He would have been in your Buryin' Beetles troop, oh, maybe five to seven years ago."

"Oh yes, I well recall young Walter. He was a...a curious Scout, intensely interested in taxidermy. But he dropped out of high school, and...Well, I'm afraid I had to ask him to hand in his Smoky Bear hat as well."

"What for? Did he get involved with hetero sex or somethin'?" she asked, hoping that might be the case. "No, no, no, not Walter. It was just that, well, I too enjoy reconstructing already dead animals, but...Well, Walter's creations—possums, foxes, and another Scout's entire litter of kittens there at the end—they were a little too, uh, lifelike. The terrified looks in their eyes, were, well, disturbing to me and the other Scouts."

Walking across Professor Lehough's front yard toward her Checker, Henrietta reckoned her mother's "gentleman friend" was not gay; reckoned that his other female "friend," Zander, might or might not have been hiding in the bathroom; and semi-worried that there might be something peculiar—maybe even dangerous—about "Walter" Bernard. At the curb, she looked back. Standing on his front porch, the professor hollered: "TELL YOUR MOTHER WE NEED TO TALK!"

Uh oh, Henrietta her own self knew from experience that "We need to talk" probably meant there really was trouble afoot in Wynona Sue's classic love story.

Twelve

While waiting for his strawberry blonde client to show up for a face-to-face in his Mr. Quickie cubicle, Max reviewed notes in a file labeled *Case of a Vamp Called Zander*. He read:

02/15/16: Following initial meeting with suspicious client, arrived 6:01 p.m. at residence of Professor Alex Lehough. Having learned in the Case of Old Folks Home Blues that an alley on the wrong side of town was a short cut to trouble, parked Mother's nondescript 1998 brown Buick on Division Street and sneaked around to the back of the bungalow. Noted lights on in a kitchen behind closed flimsy curtains. Using technique picked up from the Brad Runyon's Case of The Crooked Horse, put cocktail glass to exterior wall and pressed ear to it. Heard nothing, possibly because the glassware in this case was stemmed. Resorted to naked ear against stucco wall and...Bingo! Heard faint, muffled voices of a man and a woman! Client's suspicions about hanky-panky between Lehough, her fiance, and another dame known to her only as "Zander," were right on the money.

Kitchen lights went off. Silence followed. Moved along the back of the house. Noticed window had been broken out. Discovered the illicit lovers had cozied up in a darkened bathroom for obvious purposes. Heard Lehough, though whispering, call the babe "Honey," but then tell her he "couldn't make whoopee" that night. She started hissing like an irritated goose. Must have ankled out of the bathroom in a lather. Heard her loud voice from another room demand that Lehough "get your ass in here!"

Max silently damned the bad luck that followed. Picturing the hot-to-trot, no doubt voluptuous, no doubt brunette babe naked, spread-eagled on a red velvet living room sofa like a pulp book cover girl, he had hotfooted around the side of the house, but..."Damnit!" By the time he untangled his feet from a patch of ground ivy and finally made his way onto the bungalow's front porch—his fallen arches wouldn't tolerate gum-soled shoes, hush puppies were out of the question—well, Zander must have detected his footsteps. He faintly heard her say to Lover Boy Lehough, "Turn out the lights!" A second later the peep scene went dark. So he'd had to cheeze it.

Max pushed the gray fedora back from his forehead, leaned back in his chair, and looked at his watch. He'd not got an actual gander at Zander, and still didn't know the mysterious vamp's full name. His client, Wynona Sue, would be disappointed. But that was how the cookie sometimes crumbled. What really mattered was that he had uncovered solid proof of the elusive babe's existence. Zander was not a figment of anyone's imagination. No eyeball witness, not yet, but plenty of ear drum evidence that Lehough and Miss Zannn-derrr were doin' the Big Naughty, even though he was engaged to marry another wo-mannn.

Max sighed. Next came the hard part: Confirming the awful truth of her fiance's infidelity to his client, who...Waltzed through Mr. Quickie's front doorway and ankled toward his cubicle. She had that "Tell-me-it's-not-true" look on her face, the kind a guy sees in hospital emergency room waiting areas, in bathroom mirrors after stepping off a set of scales, and occasionally around town following an Oklahoma Sooners loss to Texas in foot-ballll. "What do you want?" she said, before sitting down across from him. "Please don't tell me you now expect to get paid for snooping."

Poor kid, probably flat broke after blowin' her hard earned dough on a wedding dress. "Like I told you—mind if I call you Wyyynona Suuue?—no charrrge." Obviously relieved, she settled into her chair, but still had that "What-do-you-want?" look on her kisser, the kind a guy gets from the saucy waitress at the Chair Crushers Cafe when he waves to her for a little busss-ing. "I'm sorry to have to tell you this, Wyyynona Suuue, but..." He gave it to her straight black: no cream, no sugar. She sat up in the chair like she'd got a caffeine jolt from a can of *Red Bullll.*

"I already know all that," the doll said, "I knew it when he stood me up for fish dinner. Alex's adulterated behavior is criminal, he ought to be shot. I might have forgiven a little fling in his past—I've already made an unrefundable deposit on a wedding dress—but now, no, not even if he gets rid of that little whore and crawls back to me. I will not settle for sloppy seconds!" Max's usual late afternoon snack came to mind. "What say we drift over to Chair Crushers for coffee and banana cream pie," he suggested. "I have a standing reservation for a cozy table, right next to the desserrrt barrr."

"No...no, it's too soon," she said, but with hesitation in her voice. "Someone might see us and think...Yes!" she said, practically jumping to her feet. "I am tired of setting at home, serving Friendly Creature highballs to Alex, watching him fall asleep, listening to him snore and mumble. To heck with him, let's have a real date, Maximo." She was a tough cookie, the kind with crust a guy had to nibble through to reach the sweet spot, and maybe worth the effff-ort.

At his regular table at Chair Crushers, an out of the way all-you-can-eat buffet joint on the west edge of town, with panoramic views of truck traffic on Interstate 40—but no beer-and-wine license—Wyyynona Suuue poured something from a flask into her cup of coffee. "Tell me a little about your-selllf," he said after downing a bite of banana cream pie. "Ever have any mannn trouble before?"

Turned out she was the typical older, sadder but --- until now—no wiser kind of dame. Married in high school to a Cajun joker, Henry Hebert—a/k/a "Ahn-REE Ay-bear"—who left her for the big city lights of Tulsa and the "big boobs of a rich whore." Married again to another wrong number who left her with nothing but bad credit and the name Walker that took years for her to get rid of. Years later, she got swept off her feet by a sooth-talking door-to-door pots-and-pans salesman, Virgil Carter, who promised to take her to Washington with him if he got elected Vice-President, but instead... She paused to take a gulp of coffee, then continued to sing like a canary dropping deeper and deeper into a coal mine of baaad luck:

Almost married a guy named Punjabi, who left her stranded in Atlantic City, New Jersey, supposedly on their way to his hometown in Pakistan "supposedly for me to meet his mother, la whore." More recently, she had been seduced by a handsome country club golf pro, "gourmet chef and French wine expert," who she thought would get rich off development of high priced Spanish mansions on the hogback west of town, but ended up working as the butler for an English princessss now living in Richmond, Virginia. Along the way, a trucker who stopped by the local bowling alley on his way to Hollywood fed her a line about making her a star, but steered his rig onto the eastbound interstate early the next morning. "And of course I have had numerous casual flings, like any attractive woman," she said, having made no mention of Professor Alex Leee-houghhh.

Poor kid, a typical hopelessly romantic broad who had read too many of those cheap "bodice busting" novels for lonely women that he'd heard about. "Actually, my grown but still quite young daughter, Henrietta, has turned into a bookworm since she enrolled in college. She's currently trying to figure out the deep mystery of my classic love stories. Believe it or not, a professor—wouldn't you know it— has planted in her silly little head a notion that all classic love stories are funny comedies. Ha! Ha! Ha! What a joke!"

While wondering who the father of "Henrietta" might be, Max felt a tingle in his pants pocket. "Sorry," he said, putting down a goo-laden fork, "gotta take this call." No doubt it was from his mother, he thought; probably she was worried that he would be late getting home to the house they shared for early supper, and another night of TV sleuthing.

"Max, it's Willis Willis," said the voice of a lawyer up in Okmulgee who in the past had occasionally engaged Max's services. "Are you by any chance working overtime at the post office? I got a small job for you." Max explained that he had retired from the postal service and now..."Too bad," said the legal fleagle, "there might have been a smoked ham in your Christmas stocking if you had come up with the info I'm lookin' for."

"Sorry," he said again to Wynona Sue, who took a nip from her flask as he reached into a jacket pocket for pad and pen. "I am still well connected with my former colleagues in the sorting room," he explained to Willis Willis, "and as a matter of fact, have set up shop as a private in-vesti-gatorrr."

"Perfecto. I've got a trot line strung down the block, and what I now know to be a big catfish nibblin'. When he makes his next move I wanna be ready to gig 'im. Know what I mean?"

Max had never fished, so had no idea what the lawyer was talking about.

"So what I need are any forwarding addresses for a gal who left town a couple of years ago. Plus any mail addressed to her that went undelivered, and might be still layin' around in that big pile out back."

Perfecto. A missing person case, Max assumed, but..."She's back in town or thereabouts, possibly living under an assumed name, but I wanna know where she's been and with who; what she's been up too while on the run; the usual nitty-gritty involved in run-of-the-mill divorce litigation."

Heck, both Mike Hammer and Phillip Marlowe avoided divorce work, but... Semi-perfecto, Max thought, putting ballpoint pen to pad. "What's the dame's name?"

"Lehough, Charlene Lehough. I expect to soon be lawyerin' for her deserted husband, a wealthy professor who lives down there in Henryetta."

Max took a deep breath and eyeballed Wynona Sue, who was pouring more of something from her flask into a glass of water. Poor kid, her fiance had been double-double timing her with two other women, one of them a wife! Would it be on the up-and-up to gumshoe for her, getting more of the goods on Lehough and the Zander babe, while also sleuthing for the naughty professor? "Sorry, Willis, I'm up to my elbows in a little after-noooner, mouthing sweet nothings, if you know what I mean. I'll have to get back to you."

"No shit. Good for you, Max. But I need to hear from you no later than first thing Monday morning."

Max looked at his watch and decided he'd better break the latest news to his unsuspecting client gently. "Alex Lehough is already married."

"Married?! Already?!" She chugalugged the glass of brownish water. Max again looked at his watch. Wynona Sue emptied the flask directly into her snoot, obviously having a hard time swallowing the hard, cold facts of in-fi-del-iteee. "The little tart, obviously young and stupid enough to have got herself knocked up, had to play the oldest trick in the book to get Alex away from me," she said, slurring her words. "It works, but believe me, not for the long haul. The ex--Mrs. Zander will be back on the street before Little Alex has stopped poopin' in his diaper."

"No, he's married to a woman named Charleeene," Max informed her. "Apparently it's been a lasting union of at leeeast two years, but..."

"Charlene?!" His client's head jolted back like she had been punched in the puss. "Alex is still married to that tramp who ran off with Virgil Carter?!"

". . . they are getting a divorce, and..."

"A divorce? Ha! About time, and then some!"

"I have been asked to find..."

"You, Maximo? You couldn't find your own ass if you searched with both hands, and that's sayin' somethin'. Charlene obviously got herself a good private peeper, one with a camera, who busted through a door and removed all doubt about Alex and that little homewrecker by catchin' 'em in fragrante! You're fired!"

Yeah, Wyyynonnna Suuue was a tough cookie alright, the kind that might break a guy's tooth—the sweet one—but still be worth nibbb-ling on. Unfortunately, however, he was running late for supper and TV at home with his mother.

Max mentally closed the *Case of a Vamp Called Zander*,

opened a new one for *Case of a Tramp Named Charlene*, and got up from his sturdy, groaning but uncrushed chair. "See you around, Sweetheart," he said to his strawberry blonde ex-client, who for some reason had put her head on the table, face down. A hardboiled parting, maybe, but he had to move on to supper and tonight's case of *Murr-derrr, She Wrote*.

Thirteen

Not knowing whether she her own self had been suspended from online college along with her rowdy classmates, Henrietta finished her homework; also unclear on why Professor LeRoy had assigned *The Romance of Tristan and Isolde.* According to the *SparkNotes* version of the "romance," a Princess Isolde who got involved with a knight named Tristan went on to marry a King Mark, who she didn't love. And then, 'stead of correcting her mistake by getting a divorce, kept on meeting Tristan at night—and making whoopee of course—in an orchard out back of the king's castle. To Henrietta, the"tale of passion and joy" sounded like not so much a "classic love story" as just another of those country and western cheatin' songs that her mother...At the thought of Wynona Sue getting cheated on again, Henrietta felt a little pang of guilt for not being more of a shoulder for her mother to cry on.

She looked at her watch. At that time of Sunday night Wynona Sue would likely be in a bathrobe, curled up on the divan in her living room, watching re-runs of her favorite TV show about wedding preparations—*Say Yes To The Dress*—all by her own self. Feeling another little pang, Henrietta went to the fridge, grabbed a big slice of left-over cherry pie, and hightailed it out of her singles-only Shangri-La apartment. On the way to the Trudgeon Street house that her mother and her had previously shared for more than twenty years, she pulled her Checker into the parking lot of E-Z Mart. A clerk at the counter told her he had sold out of red carnations—her mother's favorite—as well as bean burritos, which also would have been a comfort.

Turning onto Trudgeon Street...Hmmm? An old army jeep like she'd seen parked in Professor Lehough's driveway was setting at the curb out front of Wynona Sue's place. Intending to drive on past...What in tarnation! Henrietta slammed on the brakes and ran to the house. At the front door, her mother's mussed hair and rosy cheeks removed all doubt: The man Henrietta had seen stagger across the front yard with a brown paper grocery sack over his head could have been none other than..."I know what you're thinking," her mother said, "but Alex is only technically married to...to someone else."

Married! Married to who?

Inside, plopped onto the divan, Wynona Sue explained: "That brazen hussy—Charlene!—she's back. She's back in town, but Alex is only technically tied up. She took up with Virgil Carter almost five years ago, as everyone knows. She threw herself at Virgil, chased after him to God knows where; then followed him back to town two years ago and ran off with him! Poor Alex has been deserted twice, and been technically a lonely bachelor for years."

Her mother, seeming to think that put things to rest, got up from the divan and went into the kitchen. Henrietta noticed trampled red carnations littered under a coffee table—and bean burrito wrappings on top—but made no comment when Wynona Sue returned with a Friendly Creature highball in hand and set herself down. "Alex—you know how absent minded he can be—thought that Jezebel had divorced him long ago," she said. "Otherwise, he would never have come a-courtin', and needless to say, I would never have, uh, accepted his, uh, advances."

"But he's still married to that gal," Henrietta pointed out, "and that's legally 'technical'."

"Not for long! Oh yes, she's back again, and just you wait and see: Soon as she gets legal advice and starts collectin' so-called 'temporary' support payments, she will go through motions of trying to save the technical marriage. And try to tie things up for who knows how long. That's why Alex has agreed...has decided to beat her to the punch and get rid of her once and for all."

"Get rid of her?"

"He is hiring the county's meanest divorce lawyer first thing in the morning."

"Still, until the technical knot gets technically untied..."

"I know exactly what you mean, Henrietta. Until all that legal folderol is done with, the proper thing is for us to be, uh, discretionary about, well, you know."

Things between Henrietta and her mother got quiet as silent prayers in a church.

"Don't you understand, Henrietta: Alex Lehough got down on the floor right here where...where he mashed those flowers... and as much as proposed marriage...to me."

"Had you two been drinkin' highballs? The professor looked sorta unsteady on his feet crossin' the front yard, and drove through your neighbors' bushes while takin' his proper leave."

"How could you even suggest such a thing, Henrietta! Alex was only a little drowsy, as he has been recently, and now I know why: The poor dear gets no sleep in his own lonely bed, for worry about putting me through all this."

"What about, uh, 'Zander'? Did you happen to ask..."

"'Zander' is a dead fish. Alex couldn't come over to pick its bones that night because that...that adulteress barged back into our lives. She was the 'other woman' I overheard on the phone. Zander got ground up in the kitchen disposal, so that's the end of 'her'! Now that I know Alex's intentions... He crawled back to me, Henrietta," said Wynona Sue, with a glance at the crushed carnations, "and...Soon to be married couples have to trust each other. Aren't you happy for me?"

Henrietta went to her mother—who had started to sniffle—set down beside her on the divan and gave her a shoulder. Maybe Wynona Sue's personal love story would end up being a comedy after all. She was happy for her, but before finding the right words...Her mother straightened up, dabbed the sleeve of her bathrobe on her eyes, and said: "Honey, I hope you have learned something from all that I have been through before finding the love of my life in Alex, who was right here under by nose all along." Henrietta braced herself for a dose of motherly advice. "You better rope-and-tie that boy, Butch, before...well, no matter how unlikely it might seem ... before some other desperate old maid gets him."

After hearing her mother's "right words" for the happy occasion, Henrietta stayed speechless for a few seconds, then took her leave.

Fourteen

Early Monday morning, Alex floated on a pink cloud above the highway leading from Henryetta to Okmulgee. On his jeep's radio, never before tuned in to anything other than warnings of severe weather, music softly played. Zander was still conked out. Despite double-dosing his annoying inner voice last night before going a-courtin', he, Alex, had managed to stay awake during whoopee and...What ecstasy! Like reputedly portrayed in literary so-called love stories, he had felt a divine-like oneness with all of Nature—prominently including even Zander, oddly enough. *Wise men say/ only fools rush in*...And Wynona Sue had done him the supreme honor of accepting his proposal of marriage, on several conditions, one of which was that he get divorced from Charlene by April, absolutely no later than May. She had already bought a "Spring" wedding dress. *I can't help/ falling in love*...So late last night he'd called a lawyer, Willis V. Willis by name, and now...*Is that Elvis?* said Zander, yawning. *I thought he left the building long ago.*

"You remember Mr. Willis," Alex muttered. "He's the lawyer

who tried to strangle you after you sprung your Lone Star Tick and Alfa Gal theory from the witness box during that fossil fuel trial. "I don't want to talk about that trial anymore, so please shut up." Willis V. Willis was not the kind of man to hold a grudge. He was an unusually honorable attorney, in Alex's opinion. At their recent meeting in his office, the day after Charlene reappeared *from a cloud of sulfurous smoke*, requesting a divorce, Mr. Willis had politely insisted that he talk to almost every other lawyer in town *except the one who advertised he could "get 'er done"* and get back to him if he thought the others were too expensive. Judging by their paneled offices and fancy clothes *not to mention their bloody beaks*, indeed the other local attorneys no doubt would have been unnecessarily costly for a simple uncontested divorce. Unlike them, Mr. Willis was a humble man, *who obviously thought you too were too poor to own a clean shirt*, with whom he'd felt more comfortable *even though initially rejected for clienthood.*

Alex arrived in downtown Okmulgee and parked his jeep on Seventh Street across from the county courthouse. Inside the modest *pig sty* of Willis V. Willis, who held himself out as only a..."Git on in here, Professor," the "country lawyer" said through an open inner door from behind a large tabletop set on saw horses. "Take a load off your feet, and your shoes too. No need to put on airs around here, even though...I just wanna say, Professor, what an honor it is for me to lawyer for a Nobel Prize winnin' sumbitch. I had no idea that dang tick theory of yours would..."

"Actually, it was a 'Noble Prize'," Alex explained, after sitting down on a tractor seat screwed onto a tree stump.

"Certainly was, certainly was that. I myself am just a country lawyer. And like I say, the moral of that Lone Star Tick and Alfa Gal yarn of yours flew right over my head. I had no idea at the time…"

Alex again tried to explain that ruining the farmers' and ranchers' case against big city oil and tar interests *not to mention almost ruining their farming and ranching livelihoods* was an unintended consequence of promoting worldwide vegetarianism potentially vital to tick survival.

"Well, that duck has done flew outa the barrel. What the two of us good ol' boys are up against now is a walkin', talkin', scratchin', bitin' turducken."

Turducken? *Uh oh. Clawed feet of a turkey, gall bladder of a duck, head of a chicken!*

"Yeah, sure enough, that mean spirited, gold diggin' wife of yours has gone and hired that sumbitch, Tom Mashburn, my unscrupled bar colleague I warned you about."

"Charlene has got her own lawyer? That one down the street who calls himself 'Swifty'?"

"'Swifty', my ass. Shifty Mashburn will be milkin' your wife…"

Teats of a cow!

"…for long as it takes to make plenty of hard cheese for you, Professor. So we gotta get busy as a one-armed paperhanger with a bad case o' hives; diggin' up dirt to prove just how bad an adulteress that gal is."

"Adulteress? If you are talking about Charlene's relationship with Virgil Carter, well, she says they were just friends, and I believe her. My wife's strong religious convictions don't allow whoopee."

"Uh huh, I can see her down on her knees alright, maybe even in church, at the feet of the men's choir. And with any luck, will have pictures of her playin' the preacher's pipe organ before we're done."

"Charlene and I, we both want an amicable divorce," Alex pointed out. "Doesn't Oklahoma have a no-fault law for cases like ours?"

"Oh yeah, that's what's on the books alright. But when you get into the process of gettin' unhitched, there's no such thing as 'nobody's fault'. And judges are human too, bored most of the time, so they like a racy story to get their juices flowin' to hand out justice. Around here they're also elected. The county's church goin' voters might think their judges were not without sin their own selves if they hesitated to throw stones at women who cheat on their husbands. I've already got a private eye rummagin' for dirty laundry down in Henryetta. Soon as he's found your runaway wife's carelessly dropped undies, I'll stitch a big red 'A' smack dab in the crotch."

Alex began to think he might have been a little hasty in promising fashion-timely marriage to Wynona Sue. *Postpone the nuptials indefinitely*, Zander advised. *Wait out the shit storm of dumping the wife.*

"And by the way, Professor, while you appear to be a man likely to, well, have strong religious convictions your own self, we gotta be careful that no sauce spooned onto the goose gets splattered onto the gander. Get my meaning?"

No, Alex did not get his meaning. *No more whoopee with the hairdresser until the cow leaves home.*

"How long is this going to take?"

Willis V. Willis leaned farther back in his cowhide chair, put a shoeless—and sockless—foot on the tabletop, scratched his unshaved chin thoughtfully, and said: "Hard to say. With your wife bein' so stirred up and Shifty massaging her..."

"Charlene is 'stirred up' only to have this over with," Alex said. "When I saw her the other night, she seemed in an frightful hurry to get away from here and...possibly to get away from Virgil Carter, who may be forcing his attentions on her. She would never let anyone, uh, massage her *though the old door-to-door soft sell worked before.* And I'm not stirred up either. All I want is..."

"In a matter of weeks you'll be goin' at each other like rabid porcupines caught in the steel jaws of the same wolf trap," the country lawyer said, removing his foot from the tabletop and leaning forward with *what could only be described as a wolfish grin.* "That's just the way the same old story goes: From passion to jealousy to hate, and sometimes to..."

"It'll be past Spring by then!"

"Past Spring of next year, more like it. There's the private eye work to get done, depositions to be took from the wife, from people who know her and her reputation. Probably have to be re-took after the evidence gets stale. Shifty will be sure to take his time goin' over your financial records for the past twenty years or so, and grillin' you to tell where you're hidin' the household pots and pans. Then there's always risk of the unexpected to come up. But..."

His lawyer again leaned back. A good humored, seemingly reassuring smile crossed his jowly face. "Ever see that old movie called *Witches of Eastwick*, the one where the Devil spelled out the three Ds for what you might call sequels to love stories that only seem to have happy endings in marriage? Well, don't worry none, Professor. My best guess would be that by about, say, Christmas you'll already be well past the first D-for-Desertion and maybe halfway to the second D-for-Divorce. Now, about my fee. Before Shifty Mashburn puts a lien on your house..."

Halfway? At Christmas! *Ask him what the third D stands for, Alex. Destitution, say, might come quicker than Divorce.*

Willis V. Willis looked up from jotting something on a piece of scrap paper and gave Alex a quizzical look. "The third D is for death of a spouse," he said. "One of the unexpected things that can come up and adversely affect a divorce case. Now, about fee arrangements, I hope you and the wife have plenty of life insurance."

The office darkened. Through a large window, Alex saw that a black cloud had blotted out the sun. A bolt of lightning struck nearby with a startling crack! Ominous thunder followed. Then hard rain. Harder hail. Wind gusts shook the large window. From atop the courthouse across the street came the frightening wail of a storm warning siren. *Run for cover, Alex!* Zander screeched. *Run for our life!*

Fifteen

Since last night's news that Professor Lehough was still legally married, Henrietta had been uneasy as Aunt Hattie's stomach after a church Big Bean Supper. Not so much about whether Charlene Lehough might be inclined to go slow in getting divorced from the professor, as about what her mother might do to hurry up the process of becoming the next Mrs. Lehough. The two middle-aged gals had tangled before, from opposite corners in a love triangle involving Virgil Carter when he was running for Vice-President. Though married to the professor, it came out that Charlene and Virgil were carrying on at the same time Wynona Sue caught the eye of the smooth talking ladies man and, well, commenced to carry on with him her own self. Her mother won that cat fight, Henrietta recalled, but then tired of Virgil when the Democrat Party wired his jaw shut. Wynona Sue her own self made the deciding vote against him, stepped out of the ballot booth and on national TV told Charlene to her face: "You can have him back. I never could tolerate a mumbler." All of which struck Henrietta as what they called ironical.

Charlene got what she wanted, but now seemed to have also had her fill of Virgil's company, as well as that of the professor. Still, if she got wind of how het up Wynona Sue was to have her deserted legal husband, Henrietta doubted the current Mrs. Lehough would be inclined to return the favor and hand him over without making a fuss, or worse. Not like King Mark finally did, in a way, when he finally gave up spitefully trying to keep Princess Isolde and Sir Tristan apart. Determined to speak up in class and ask why a tale about an Irish princess and an English knight sneaking around—like a local hairdresser and insects professor—Henrietta opened her laptop.

Ah, The Romance of Tristan and Isolde, Professor LeRoy said in type, *a tale of Passion and Joy most sharp, and Anguish without end, and Death!*

He went on to re-cap the story about how Sir Tristan, a gallant English knight in the service of King Mark of Cornwall, was victorious but wounded in combat against an invading Irish knight, then sailed to Ireland to claim Isolde's hand for his king; how Isolde, a beautiful Irish princess, went to his bedside intending to kill him and avenge his slaying of her betrothed, but instead nursed him back to good health; and how on their way back to England, where Isolde was supposed to marry King Mark, they unwittingly drank a magic potion brewed by her mother for Isolde and the king.

Isolde's nurse and friend, Brangaine, came upon them; she saw them gazing at each other in silence as though ravished and apart; she saw the pitcher she had brought to them by mistake; she snatched it up and cast it into the shuddering sea and cried aloud: "Isolde, and Tristan, you have drunk death together." And then from the opera version, perhaps the most dramatically romantic words ever spoken or sung on page or stage:

"Tristan!" said Isolde in a trembling voice.

"Isolde!" said Tristan, overwhelmed with emotion.

Any questions, Ms. Hebert? You appear to be the only student in class today.

Death? I thought it was a love potion they drank, Henrietta typed.

Death is often seen in classic literature as romantic love's ultimate achievement of lost wholeness, as in Romeo and Juliet. That's why ecstatic orgasm and that glimpse of the divine it brings is called 'the little death'. If Adam and Eve had not taken forbidden fruit from the Logos Tree and mixed its juice with that of fruit from the Eros Tree, they would have remained physically immortal. Ecstatic orgasm in the arms of another takes us momentarily back to the Garden of Eden and the feeling—just as God said—that we are God.

My name is William, by the way, but please call me Bill, "Bill W." if you like (lol). Are you at least eighteen years of age and single, Henrietta?

To change the subject, Henrietta asked why some people said *The Romance of Tristan and Isolde*, not the story of Adam and Eve, was the first love story.

Good question. Probably in part because it was told and sung by troubadours in common taverns across France and Britain, and put lusty flesh and bone on the love story's conceptual framework. In those medieval times, the dominant notion of romantic love was that of the so-called courtly kind practiced by the aristocracy. Flirtatious, verbally passionate, but amounting mostly to secret exchanges of sentiments and tokens of affection such as hankies and gloves. Isolde introduced liberated female sexuality and made real what had been only an idea of romantic love. I was born under the sign of the Fish, Henrietta. I hope you are not an incompatible (lol) Virgo?

Henrietta ignored the personal question. *But Isolde and*

Tristan carrying on was against the rules, she protested, *and done right under King Mark's nose behind his back.*

As was the carrying on of Adam and Eve, the professor answered, *behind God's back. In fact, the linkage between the Garden of Eden and the orchard beneath the balcony of Tintagel Castle where the adulterous couple trysted is the subject of a treatise of mine that...*As Professor LeRoy went on to "explain" Tristan's and Isolde's voyage from Ireland as returning to the Garden of Eden—through ecstatic orgasm again—Henrietta began to miss the company of Agnetta, Barbara Jean and Charlie Morrison. She also forgot her other questions and got back to feeling uneasy about the fix her mother was in.

When hazel and honeysuckle continued to grow from Tristan's and Isolde's side-by-side graves and intertwine, King Mark gave up trying to chop out the vines. He forgave the two lovers, having not the "rage of love to hatred turned...nor fury of a woman scorned," so to speak. Not to be sexist, but cherchez la femme in your literary studies, Ms. Hebert. Cherchez la femme!

Do you, by chance, have dark hair and dark eyes?

When Mr. Harold bobbed into the office later, Henrietta indirectly brought up her concern about what Mrs. Lehough might do if she caught the professor over on Trudgeon Street with his head stuck inside a grocery sack, and also asked about "Professor Bill's" warning.

"Cherchez la femme?" said her educated boss. "Well, a literal translation would be 'look for the woman', but in certain contexts it could be taken as a warning to 'look out for the woman'. As for the Lehoughs' situation, well, divorce is always a sad thing, the very antithesis of the classic love story in some cases. And when those danged lawyers take charge, sure enough: Love to hatred can turn on a dime."

Dang it, her mother putting up Professor Lehough to hire the meanest divorce lawyer in the county was asking for trouble. Heck, the professor was likely down to about his last dime already. If Wynona Sue and him would just lay low—not together—like sleeping dogs, Henrietta reckoned that Charlene Lehough would more likely not delay getting legally unhitched from the husband she had deserted years ago.Unless Charlene Lehough held a grudge against him, or got wind of her stranged husband being so het up to re-marry, she would likely be all for getting unhitched from him by now. Hmmm?

Sixteen

At exactly 3:01 p.m. on Monday, Charlene's lifeline to salvation went stone cold dead. In a fit of frustration, she hurled the cheap cell phone against a wall of her crummy room at the Fountainblue Motel, where she had been holed up for three days and nights since meeting with so-called "Swifty" Mashburn. Fra Guido was close at hand—she imagined she could smell the familiar moldy odor of his monk's cowl—and her divorce case against Alex was grinding justice way too slowly, she sensed. On the phone this morning, her legal shyster told her that Alex's legal shyster—that cornball son of a bitch, Willis V. Willis—was making progress unnecessarily difficult. Swifty suggested they meet in person to plot a next move, but then put her on hold to take another call. That was six hours ago. With a sinking feeling that yet again she had been double-crossed by a man who valued only her dirty mind, Charlene went to a window, peeked through a crack in the room's ratty drapes, and sighed in despair.

The motel owner's teenaged son, "Hughie," would soon be home from school, making his daily round of collecting the next day's room rent. Obscenely snickering, the horny adolescent punk would again not so subtly hint that her delivery of another cheap thrill would be acceptable in lieu of cash. Charlene closed the the crack of light from the outside world and turned away from the window into utter gloom. She couldn't take it anymore. Corruption of a so-called minor's so-called morals could get her arrested. In jail, she would be a sitting duck for the Fra or some other C02 Gang thug already inside the walls. And she was tired; her repertoire of dirty jokes to turn on Hughie's sexual fantasies was exhausted, the barrel of bawdy limericks almost empty. There was only one way out of her desperate, tawdry existence, and that was to kill herself.

Charlene immediately went to work on executing the plan of last resort she had concocted during the past weekend while lying on the stained cover of the motel's saggy bed, smoking her last pack of cigarettes and catching up with the Kardashians in black-and-white TV re-runs of shows she had missed. From a three-year-old magazine about corn, she tore out bits of print. From cracks and crannies in the crumbling tile floor of a shower cubicle, she used her fingernails to scratch out sticky goo. From the drawer of a wobbly nightstand, she retrieved an ancient postcard depicting the Fountainblue Motel back in it's *Free Ice Water!* better days. On the backside of the postcard, she pasted a note:

cHARlenE LEhoUgh is DEaD I mURdered heR
4 WHat sHE Did 2 U MAY shE R I P 4 EVerMor
A FRieNd

That ought to throw off Fra Guido and any other hooligan hired by criminal climate change Deniers, she thought, before going on to paste an address in a space to the right of her message.

Hurriedly, Charlene then put on the black burka and skulked out of the Fountainblue flop house.

At the local post office fifteen minutes later, she counted out coins to buy a stamp, stuck the postage on the postcard, turned away and..."Lehough, Charleeene Leee-hough," said a man's voice from behind her. She wheeled around... "or Mrs. Alexander Leee-houghhh. Last known address: 1524 Division Streeet." She had never seen the Fra not wearing a coarse brown cowl, and hadn't recognized the man's drawling voice that had uttered her name as the Fra's, but...No, the excessively broad-in-the-beam man on the other side of the stamp counter—his back turned to her, his head covered by a gray felt hat, dressed in a pinstriped suit with old fashioned padded shoulders—was obviously a different oil-and-tar gangster, sent to kill...In terror, Charlene ran from the post office.

On the sidewalk outside, she looked right and left, searching for a free-standing mailbox. Finally, she saw a receptacle for the Hail Mary postcard about a half block down Main Street. She made a run for it, but from behind her...*Clomp! Clomp! Clomp!*

At the mailbox..."Lookin' for this?" said the somewhat less deepish, now out-of-breath voice of the fat man she'd overheard at the post office. She turned to face him, expecting to see a dagger pointed at her pounding heart, but..."Left it on the counter," he said, with not a knife, but her postcard in a hammy hand. "Hmmm?" he hmmmed, looking down at what she had pasted on the card. "To 'Boone Oil and Tar Trucking Co. in OKC'." He put the card into a mailbox slot, eyed her up and down as though sizing up a smoked turducken to take home for dinner, and said, "I think you better come along with me, Sweetheart."

Out of a terrified daze fifteen minutes or perhaps hours

later, Charlene found herself seated at a restaurant table. The mysterious portly man sat across from her, eating from a hunk of banana cream pie. A huge serving of some kind of pudding overflowed a bowl set in front of her. Famished, she threw off the burka hood and dug into what she believed must be a kind of last supper before her mob-style execution, for which she would have preferred something less fattening.

"So you're a blonde," said her captor. "Yeah, dead ringer for the hitch-hiking babe—wearing only a raincoat just like yours—who Mike picked up one night in the *Case of Kiss Me, Deadly*. Inside the car, the dame in distress was incoherent, again just like you; talkin' like a luuunatic escaped from a funny farm. Abducted by two thugs and later..."

"Who are you?" she asked. "What are you going to do to me? Please, I was not the one who took the side of the farmers and ranchers, not me! I am a devout climate change Denier. I swear!"

"Don't worry, Honey, I'm not gonna let myself get knocked semi-unconscious like Mike did. And to level with you, I'm not hardboiled enough to watch two goooombahs torture a beautiful blonde to death without blacking out all the way."

That was somewhat reassuring, but... "Dollar to a donut," he said, "mannn trouble?"

"Yeah, the story of my life," she answered, pushing away the emptied bowl. "How do you happen to know so much about me, Mister...?"

"Maximo's the name, private detection's my game," he said, spooning a gob of gooey pie filling toward his mouth "In the company of innocent young dames like you, I call myself a private Richarrrd. Whatta they call you, Sweetheaaart?"

To explain the burka, "Kardashian" came to mind. "Kasandra Kardashian." Charlene was beginning to feel oddly comfortable with the strange corpulent character, who then unbuttoned his double breasted suit jacket to reveal… a plastic water pistol in a shoulder holster. Catching her sidelong glance, he said, "Don't worry, Honey, old junior doesn't squirt lead unless it's ab-so-lute-ly nec-ess-sarry."

As "Maximo" got up and waddled toward a dessert bar, Charlene regained her full wits. He seemed to be not a Fra Guido type after all, but she had distinctly overheard him inquiring about her—"Charlene Lehough"—at the post office. When he returned with a second plate of the same dessert snack, "Lucky for me you came along," she said. "Did you just 'come along' or—I notice you're not wearing a wedding ring, Maximo—were you, by chance, on the lookout for an innocent dame in distress like me?"

"Strictly business that we happened to cross paths," he said, digging in. "I'm working a mysterious *Case of a Tramp Named Charlene*. Bloodhounding a runaway adult-er-esss. Not much to go on except name, and the skinny I got on the phone today from the deserted husband, an absentminded Professor Leee-hooough. Poor sap, all he could remember about the hot-to-trot broad was height between five and six feet, like you; dark brown eyes, like yours; but bruuunetttte. And inclined to have a baaad temper, especially toward defenseless household pets. So you can see why I'm packing old junior, just in case I happen to cross paths with the two-timing tramp some night in a blind alley."

Alex and Maximo, what a pair. Charlene could never have imagined "crossing paths" with anyone else as clueless as her estranged husband. How dare the son of a bitch remember hardly anything about her!

"Maximo, I'm flat broke," she said, sliding a hand across the table, "and I can't go back to the flea bag I've been staying in. But if you would like to hear some dirty jokes and limericks in the back seat of your car..."

"The snack is on me, Sweetheart," he said, taking her hand in his beefy paw. "I pegged you for a dame down on her luck, which is why I picked you up. What say I take you to the bus station, buy you a ticket back home to mama?"

"Gee, thanks, Max, but I can't go home to...to Kansas. I'm on the run from a guy...my boyfriend from back in high school. Guido—that's his name—has turned, uh, into a hood, and won't leave me alone." Charlene squeezed his hand. "And besides, I think I might like it here. Maybe I'll get a job scrubbing floors and..."

"Bingo!" he said. "Since I started workin' full days, my mother has been on me to keep up with chores around the house, and no doubt I'll be on stake outs lots of nights for awhile. What say you move into the garage apartment, lend a hand with the cooking and keep Mom company 'til you get back on your feeet?"

Bingo! As a once somewhat innocent young girl, Charlene had dreamed of a knight in shiny armor coming to her rescue, never imagining, however, that he would be so stupid, and way too "heavyset" to ride a horse.

Seventeen

Henrietta put down her eye-phone, stood up from her *Weekly Herald* desk, looked up at the ceiling and counted to ten. Her needy mother's up-and-down romance with Professor Lehough had become one of those tiresome soap operas. She her own self was, if anything, glad that the undivorced current love of Wynona Sue's life had not come a-courting since Sunday, with or without a sack over his head. She did not care that her mother's boyfriend had turned "stand offish." Dang it, except for Butch Bernard, she her own self had lately had no male company. With a sigh, Henrietta went to the rest room to look in a mirror. Hmmm? Her hair was still thick and naturally strawberry blonde. Her face was the same as it was in high school when most thought she was not ordinary to look at. Boys and men supposedly cottoned to cornflower blue eyes. She was not completely flat chested, but... Heck, if today she was again the only one in class, Henrietta had a notion to flirt back at Professor "Bill W." and—even though he was likely to be a dirty-minded old man—maybe even invite him to come a-courtin' her. She was that desperate.

Back at her desk, she opened her laptop and again sighed. So far, her liberal arts education about so-called classic love stories had only made her frustrated as a spinster about what she her own self was missing. So in a way it was a mercy that todays's assignment was the tale of *Othello* by William Shakespeare. For a "Moorish" army general to believe wicked gossip about his wife sneaking around with another man, and kill her in a fit of uncorrect jealousy, was not a love story in her book. She dreaded going to class, but…

Professor LeRoy:

I had intended to dive directly into the sometimes dark side of the classic love story today, but now that attendance is back to normal and in light of recent classroom events, I have decided to instead step outside the box of literature per se and look at our subject from a somewhat abstract, perhaps less controversial angle, to-wit: That of Dr. Carl Jung's brilliant insights into romantic love and 'storytelling'. Dr. Jung, a psychologist, demonstrated that the unconscious human mind is occupied by a number of universal archetypes from which images emerge as what might be called characters shaped by mankind's shared history and culture as well as by each person's personal context: The brave hero, the damsel in distress, the boogeyman. So too do archetypes include classic story lines such as the journey, the flood, the switcheroo, that unconsciously shape our perceptions of worldly events and, our behavior.

Foremost among these archetypes is the feminine anima of the male unconscious mind and the masculine animus in the unconscious of women. Guess what the most archetypal tale is? The classic love story! Boy meets girl, boy loses girl, boy gets girl back—a famous movie maker famously insisted—is the only plot. And so an entire generation grew up on motion picture love stories with happy endings. These and other outward manifestations of the divine romance reflect what takes place in each persons' unconscious as he and she innately strives for a regained sense of wholeness, that Jung called individuation. In real life—without concious rhyme or reason—man projects his anima, woman projects her animus, onto a member of the opposite sex, who becomes perceived in his or her eyes as what? His or her soul mate! Think of Adam and Eve, Psyche and Eros, Tristan and Isolde. Intense feelings of love occur, sometimes with equally intense feelings of jealousy— "the error bred in the bone to be loved alone," to quote a certain poet—and those feelings sometime cross a thin line between love and hate. It's the same old story: The fundamental things apply, as time goes by.

So let's now turn to the third of the foremost archetypes, to-wit: That of the same-sex shadow.

Barbara Jean Booker:

There you go again: Same old homo hate bias against same-sex romance as something "dark."

Agnetta Hurley:

Yeah, and next comes the Othello story: Same old racist bias against black men as "shadows."

Professor LeRoy:

You may be right, though Dr. Jung demonstrated that we all carry a shadow within us. I myself agree with most who for centuries have regarded the man Othello as a tragic hero—victim of alienation between Eros and Psyche inside him—and his classic love story the most romantic of Shakespeare's plays. "He loved perhaps not wisely but too well. His hand, like that of the base Indian, threw away a pearl richer than all his tribe."

Agnetta Hurley:

Trigger! Now you're disrespecting Native Americans!

Barbara Jean Booker:

Yeah, Shakespeare has the dark-skinned "hero" murder his pearly-white wife. Whatta love love story!

Charlie Morrison:

Some murder mystery. I saw it was the Death Shadow, out to eat my brain, soon as he said "Haply for I am black," just like in Persona 3.

Professor LeRoy:

What you say only proves what Jung said: Archetypes are in part deposits of the constantly repeated experiences of humanity; a collective unconscious embedded with a kind of readiness to produce over and over again the same or similar mythical ideas in stories and in real life. Other than "Othello," there have been many non-homophobic, non-racist classic love stories in literature—probably also in Play Station games—involving devastating results of jealousy arising from the archetypal Eternal Triangle. Mark Anthony-Cleopatra-Caesar... King Arthur-Guinevere-Sir Lancelot... The entire One Thousand and One Arabian Nights tales told by Scheherazade to King Shahryar were to distract him from killing her on their honeymoon, as he had done to numerous other wives rather than risk a repeat of the humiliation caused by the sexual infidelity of his first Missus.

Agnetta Hurley:

Trigger! Dark skinned Moors like the king scare me.

Barbara Jean Booker:

He's a serial killer of women, like we were farm animas!

Aganetta Hurley:

That's why I am almost a vegetabletarian, except for pork chops... fried chickens...and livers.

Professor LeRoy:

In the Othello story, the clash of wild, uncontrollable Eros and his Soul was triggered by jealousy, but that is not the only human foible that can cause such devastating conflict, and Eros is not always the real "villain," as we shall see. In closing, I suggest you ponder the last words uttered by Othello's wife and soul mate, Desdemona. Asked who killed her, Desdemona's dying words were, "nobody, I myself."

Class dismissed.

Henrietta closed her laptop, put "Othello" out of her mind, and went back to stewing over her own unromantic situation. She'd had other semi-serious boyfriends since Gaylord gave her the mitten. Bobby Lowry, though a college graduate, begged her to wear his Phi Lambda Epsilon high school fraternity pin. Billy O'Dell courted her in a graveyard up near Tulsa that he was secretly digging up at night, as it turned out, so that his mother could later replace the bodies with a lifestyle shopping center. A handsome undercover narc agent, assigned to bust up a drug ring located in one of the town's abandoned coal mines, seriously sparked her. An also handsome climate change lawyer from Washington, D.C. and a real cute cowboy storm chaser named Rowdy Travis from Yukon, Oklahoma pert near fought over her. More recently, Chip Wilkie, a shortish but semi-unordinary looking fella—who majored in Golf at Harvard University and was in town to run a tournament—had invited her to visit him in the far hills of New Jersey.

But it now looked like "The Romance of Sir Gaylord and Princess Henrietta"—in which there had been some ecstatic orgasms alright—was likely the only classic love story she would ever be a character in. Her inner masculine "animus" seemed to be permanently stuck onto Gaylord. Why? What was it that made someone see only a particular other as her or his "soul mate"? That was the "mystery" of the classic love story, Henrietta reckoned. As for figuring it out, she still felt dumb as a watch dog barking at a tree knot.

Eighteen

Max paced back and forth in his Mr. Quickie cubicle like a hungry walrus, two steps in one direction, two steps backward in the other. He was beginning to understand why both Mike Hammer and Phillip Marlowe avoided divorce cases, even though he'd read that the term "private detective" first appeared in connection with a matter of marital mystery back in 1869 — *Case of He Knew He Was Right*— handled by a gumshoe named Sam Bozzle. Probably like shooting a fish in a barrel compared to his own current *Case of a Tramp Named Charlene,* which was an en-ig-maaa. Charlene Lehough had left no forwarding address, and no other traces of her prior local existence except a lingering odor of cheap perfuuume. Sure, plenty of married dames rode stray boloney ponies these days, but ordinarily in out-of-the-way motel bedroom rodeos not advertised to the general public. Charlene, on the other hand, had made no secret of dancing in the sheets with a joker named Virgil Carrr-terrr. Everyone in town seemed to know she had been sampling his rhubarb over the back fence long before she ran off with him about two years ago. In fact...

Max paused wearing out the office carpet, picked up the notes from yesterday's stroll down Main Street, and read: *Young good looking skirt, Henrietta Hebert, investigative reporter for Weekly Herald, reported seeing the Lehough broad and Carter in courthouse lobby on day of "climate change trial." In company of robed cleric. Assumed they had picked up marriage license when the padre tied their hands together with rope. The witness' nose seemed as out of joint as the bent schnoz of a dame who had been the bride's romantic rival.*

No record of holy bedlock license issued, but client's runaway wife, Charlene, is clearly guilty as sin of at least adultery and possibly bigamy. Abandoned husband's divorce case sewn up tight. Case closed.

But to the mouthpiece, Willis Willis, all that was not enough evidence of monkey business. On the phone, the legal fleagle had said that short of photos showing the wife and Carter actually stuffin' the muffin, he needed proof of cohabitation to cinch the case for the two-timing dame's public stoning in court. Hmmm? Willis Willis was obviously the kind of sharp lawyer that usually angry broads went to see when they wanted a pound or two of ground spouse.

So earlier today Max had taken a bus to Virgil Carter's nearby hometown of Dewar, where beneath the en-ig-maaa of the *Case of the Tramp Named Charlene*, he'd come up against what could only be called a per-plex-ing rid-dllle. At the post office there, a former colleague confided that Carter had not only filed a forwarding address for a P. O. Box in Domino, Texas, but regularly called to check on delivery status of disability checks and lifetime subscriptions to girly magazines. What a loser. After an hour of two of sleuthing, he located Carter's mother—old, wrinkled, wrong size dentures, but still with youthful jet black hair—living in a house trailer. Again Max paused from pacing to refer to the case notes:

2/17/16: Mother Carter unhappy that she has not received support payments in years for wayward son's six kids, and that his ex-wives won't cop to maternity. In answer to question about her knowledge of any recent romantic relationship involving her wayward boy, she said he would not survive more than 24 hrs. without constant care from a woman. What a wimp. But in answer to follow-up question, no way: Carter would never grind corn off the cob with any floozie who had dark hair. (Note that Charlene Lehough is known to be a lifelong brunette.)

Max had a feeling ham for Christmas was barely still on his client's shopping list. So now, having already missed his regular afternoon snack, he continued to pace back and forth, waiting for the postmaster serving Domino, Texas to return his call. Near collapse for lack of a sugar fix... His cell phone buzzed.

"Whatta you want?" a voice growled. "We're shorthanded around here, so make it fast." Max introduced himself as a postal service veteran who well understood how busy..."Oh well, that's different," said the Texas comrade-in-arms in a friendly tone. "Never too busy to chew the fat with another one of the few, the proud, the brave who's been out all day in snow, rain, heat and gloom, swiftly completing his appointed rounds. How's the weather up there? Nice, lazy, almost Spring-like day down here."

"Retreated from the front line years ago," Max felt obliged to admit. "Dogs got to barking so bad I could hardly ankle from one mailbox to another," he explained, referring to his feet. "The will was there, but the waaayyy..."

"Wish I had the guts to chicken out. Down here we're now fighting off coyotes, raccoons, and rattlesnakes in addition to dogs, rabid kids, and old farts who blame us for lost Social Security checks. Must be that global warming that's got 'em stirred up."

After another thirty minutes or so of swapping war stories, Max got straight to the point: "Trackin' a skunk, name of Virgil Carrr-terrr. Ring a bell?"

"Get in line. Must be dozens of bill collectors, unhappy worn-out tire customers and pissed off girlfriends lookin' all over for ol' Virgil since he woke up and walked out of the hospital Sunday night. Docs thought he was a goner—not enough insurance for brain surgery parts and labor—but twenty-four hours after they found a lead plate to put in his head—engraved to him for outstanding cookware sales back in aught-four—well, I guess you could say the Docs were right. Ol' Virgil is a goner, in a way, which is a miracle after what happened to him."

"Let me guess: Bill collect-orrrs and needy girlfriends in hot pursuit. Flim-flammer blew a tiiire. Lost controlll. Hit a treee."

"Nope. Somebody swatted his head with the butt of a shotgun by the look of things; wrapped him in duct tape and left ol' Virgil to die a slow death out there on the Flying Feathers spread. Doc says turducken was not a factor, so that's a relief."

After learning what a turducken was, Max made a mental note to order three in case an extra ham didn't make the Morgan family's Christmas dinner menu; then zeroed in: "Any suspicion it might have been a certain dame—bruuunette named Char-leeene—who did the dirty deeed?"

"No, but maybe yes. A gal ol' Virgil was shacked up with out there—went by 'Jenny Cooper', for what that's worth—has skedaddled alright. But she's a blonde, except from time to time at the roots."

After getting a description of Carter—black hair like his mother, glasses, big nose and black mustache—Max ended the call and hmmmed. The *Case of the Tramp Named Charlene* had proved to be an en-ig-ma wrapped in a rid-dllle wrapped in a mys-ter-y possibly involving at least attempted murrr-derrr. Needless to say, he was intrigued. But then, stomach rumblings reminded him it was time to head home for supper with his mother and that stray kid they had taken off the streets, Kasandra Kardashian. Driving to the house...Kardashian? Kardashian? Kardashian?...He'd heard the obviously Irish name before, but couldn't say where or when. Not that it mattered. To both him and his mother the babe was now just Sandy—short and sweet for Kasandra—which also almost rang a bell. Sandy? Sandier? Sandiest?

"Well, it's about time," his mom had said when he brought the Jane home yesterday, only a few minutes late for supper. "I'm proud of you, Maxie," she said, which was strange in a way. Out of her black outfit and into one of his mother's house dresses, Sandy had turned out to seem not exactly the kind of dame a guy took home to meet his mom. Truth be told, he'd not initially pegged her for the type of hitch hiker Mike picked up in the *Case of Kiss Me, Deadly*; not 'til the babe took off the hood of her rain gear and he saw she was a blonde did he connect those dots. No, his first impression had been that Sandy was likely a redheaded hooker, such as the broad Mike rescued at a diner one night in the *Case of My Gun Is Quick*. That doll was also on the lam from an badass boyfriend. Mike roughed up the creep, shoved old junior in his mug and told him to scram. Handed three fifties to the fluff, but...Max let out a long sigh. There was no way to get around it: Mike made a mistake by not escorting the redhead to the bus station. The next day he found out she was dead, supposedly run over by a bus, but no way: It was murrr-derrr.

Immediately after opening the back door to the house he'd

lived in all his life, Max detected the aroma of fried chicken, one of his many favorites. In the kitchen, he saw his mother mashing a big bowl of potatoes, also a favorite. "Max, it's a special occasion," she announced. "Since noon there's been a *Murder, She Wrote* marathon on TV. Go on in there and keep Sandy company. That poor little thing—I got her some clothes today at the Walmart, size ten!—so we've got to fatten her up for... Go on to the living room, she must be lonely." In the hallway, he detected the smell of cigarette smoke. Hammer, Marlowe, Spade, even Brad Runyon dragged on butts, of course, but in modern movies and on TV, the sight of anyone lighting up was a sure tip-off he or she was a baaad act-orrr.

"Those fags will kill you," he said to Sandy, lounging in his mom's living room recliner. Decked out in a navy blue sailor suit, with a red ribbon stuck on the top of her spiked almost white hair, she looked like the kind of prize a guy would bring home to mother, maybe after winning a pie eating contest at the county faaair. "Ahoy, Maxie," she said with a wave, "drop anchor and join the party," which he did. "Been watching Jessica Fletcher solve tricky cases all day," she said, "and Mom's right: Jess is too skinny, but you really do look a lot like her." Max had long ago written off his mother's comparison as based on nothing more than her often expressed disappointment that he had not been born a girl. J.B. Fletcher wasn't so hot. Within seconds of leaning back in his recliner, Max detected that the *Case of Twice Dead* was playing on the TV screen, which wasn't really even a murder mystery. "The brilliant professor faked his death," he informed Sandy. "The prime suspect is innocent. Any sharp shamus would have solved this so-called case of non-murrr-derrr in ten seconds."

"Speaking of professors," said Sandy, "why did your client,

uh, Professor Lehough, go to the expense of hiring you to track down the runaway 'adulteress'? Does he want to kill her as payback for, you know, banging another guy?"

"Lehough is a client once re-moooved. I work for his mouthpiece, Willis Willis. Run of the mill divorce case: Guys and dolls fall out of love, start fighting to the death over the household pots and pans."

"Pots and pans?"

"Lawyer lingo for marital assets, and the professor apparently has a jaaack-pot stashed somewhere."

"I wonder where? Think you could find where your client 'once removed' hid the 'pots and pans'?"

"Oh yeah, I could score 'em in a New York minute, but by then the lawyers would likely have emptied the pot of gold into their own pock-ets. That's the way the cookie crumbles in the divorrrce gammme."

Max's mother came in with a tray of chow that would have done the Chair Crushers joint proud in terms of weight; hurried back to the kitchen and returned with a man-size meal for him. By the time she herself was seated for supper on a wood bench... "Oh goody," Mom said to Sandy, "this is the one that had Max stumped. At fourteen years of age, he didn't understand how a woman's hanky panky would be cause for blackmail," she semi-whispered. "He's still kind of retarded when it comes to the subject of s-e-x."

The Case of Tough Guys Don't Die started, as always, with the murder of a P.I. named Archie Miles, whose surviving partner helped Jessica ultimately solve the simple whodunnit. Max felt compelled to point out that back in 1989, at age fourteen, he'd spotted right off that the dead gumshoe's name was strangely like that of Sam Spade's partner in the *Case of The Maltese Falcon*, namely Miiiles Arrrcher. A sharp-eared private Richard notices things fishy about naaames.

"Don't be fooled, Sweetheart," he then warned Sandy. "It was an inside job. The staff person stole the sexy client's file with intent to blaaack-maiiil." She thanked him for the tip. Through the evening, over multiple slices of pie topped with ice cream covered in various flavored sauces, he continued to walk the wide-eyed babe through, first the *Case of What You Don't Know Can Kill You*, then *Case of The Dead Letter*, next the duck-soup *Case of The Tainted Lady*. And finally, one of his favorites, the *Case of Murrrr-derrr a la Mode*.

The poor kid—must have had a rough day—seemed have nodded off at some point along the way, just like his mom on the bench. When he shook Sandy awake…Uh oh, Max saw it clear as mud in her eyes: The size-ten platinum blonde broad was falling for him, hard, and that almost always spelled T-R-O-U-B-L-E.

Nineteen

In a nightmare, Henrietta dreamed she was running from someone, maybe Butch Bernard. But then her Cajun Grandma Hebert started yelling "run, Sadie, run," and she suddenly realized she had become a thirty-five-year-old spinster named Sadie Hawkins—"the homeliest gal in Dogpatch," according to her grandma—chasing after someone, maybe Butch Bernard. She woke up in a sweat. Butch had called her three or four times, wanting to "shoot pool" and talk about the robot project he had in the works. But having got Professor Lehough's report about "Walter" getting kicked out of his Scout troop, she had put him off. Now she reconsidered. Butch had mentioned that Roy Potter—supposedly a high-tech "whiz kid"—was helping him "get 'er done," and Roy was Police Chief Potter's teenaged boy. She had run across him out at the town dump that night when he and Professor Lehough's "Buryin' Beetles" Scout Troop were making plans to start a "yuteful" revolution against their elders. Their mischief had amounted to nothing much more than setting off a few cherry bombs and...Dang it, her chances of locating a boyfriend in her little ol' hometown were thin as thirsty cattle. Probably there was no real reason for her to feel uneasy about Butch. It was broad daylight. He wasn't likely to do any harm to her or anyone else...'cept maybe kittens.

Thirty minutes later, she took a deep breath and pushed open the old fashioned wood door of the Bernard family garage. There set Butch at a table, head bent over a laptop. Next to him—land sakes alive—there stood a robot, five feet tall, tin head square as a cracker box, with bright red wax lips stuck on its face. Butch looked up through his real thick glasses, blinked, then broke into a big grin. "Hey, Henrietta, meet Salome," he said, moving over next to "her," one of his *Metal Soul Mates*, she reckoned. "I was just readin' an online article that says one out of four females in England between ages eighteen and thirty-four would be happy to date a robot." Henrietta, though desperate for a date her own self, was dubious. "Both of my Japanese customers are old men and not so picky," he explained, "but...Salome is an upgrade of Samantha: You know, that operating system with artificial female intelligence that Theodore Twombley—in that movie called *Her*—put into his regular ol' computer so they could just talk to each other. Roy programmed Salome's OS to whisper in Mr. Ito's ear like Samantha did to Theodore. Wanna see her do her sexy thing?"

Butch went back to the laptop. The robot's red eyes lit up. "What does a baby computer call its father?" said a squeaky voice from inside the square head. "Data."

"Yuk, yuk, yuk," Butch yucked. "That's just to break the ice. Now comes the sexy lines that Roy got from his great grandma, who is a hundred years old and an expert on the Bible and classic love movies." Henrietta watched and listened. "Is that a gun in your pocket, or are you just glad to see me?" Salome asked.

"When I'm good, I'm very good, and when I'm bad I'm better. Just whistle, you know how to whistle don't you, Mr. Ito. Just pucker your lips and...blow. A hard man is good to find," the robot then said, as an arm and attached metal claw started to slowly jerk up and down like, well, like Salome was programmed to give Mr. Ito a hand job. "Emotion in motion is like the game of Bridge," it whispered, jerking faster. "If you don't have a good partner, you better have a good hand."

Henrietta was shocked. "Roy Potter's great grandma passed on to him all that from the Bible and old love movies?!"

"I know, I know," Butch said, it's too old fashioned even for old Japanese men. "Listen to these lines Roy got from his younger grandma and mother." He typed something on his keyboard and the sexy robot said, "You're not very smart—I like that in a man. I don't bite...unless it's called for. Take me to bed or lose me forever. I have crossed oceans of time to find you. You complete me."

"Better," Henrietta said, just to be polite, "but..."

"I know, I know," Butch said, before turning off the robot's eyes and coming over to her. "Mr. Ito sent Sally back, C.O.D. Roy and me are just no darn good at sexy girl talk, which is why we need you, Henrietta, to help us upgrade her. You said you were a college expert on the classic love story, and that's just what the project needs."

"Well, I don't know. The thing is, Butch, a talking, jerking metal robot strikes me as kinda..."

"I know, I know," he said again. "The article about young English gals admitted that for them a robotic boyfriend would have to be 'a perfect match' and look like a real-life human being. I reckon even old Mr. Ito feels about the same. So me and Roy are going to upgrade Salome into an humanoid, like Ava in that other movie that came out last year. The one called *Ex Machina*. Roy and you will re-program her OS and I will come up with some bones for a rounder head, gentler hands, and some kind of skin. It would be funner than grafting cats paws onto a rooster," he continued. "We could, you know, 'play pool' again on your divan, say things at each other this time, and stop to put the good lines into my laptop. Yuk, yuk, yuk."

Henrietta looked at her watch, lied that she needed to hurry off to class, and told Butch she would have to think about helping him and Roy satisfy old Mr. Ito. In a flash, she'd realized that what she really needed to think about—serious as blocked arteries this time—was getting out of the bottom of the barrel she was in by escaping from her little ol' hometown.

Twenty

By the time Alex reached the Trudgeon Street sidewalk in front of Wynona Sue's modest little house—having walked several blocks at an unhurried pace so as to not draw anyone's attention—he was in a sweat. The rented hazmat suit he wore was virtually unventilated. *You look ridiculous, Alex*, said Zander. Tanks strapped to his back seemed to have gotten heavier. *You of all people, decked out as Otto the Orkin Man, serial killer of insects!* "It's only sugared water," he mumbled, now squirting the sweet treat around the edges of Wynona Sue's front porch with a long metal wand tipped with a nozzle. *Who was it who said a man with an erection will go into places he otherwise wouldn't dare to enter with a bazooka?* "Stifle the dirty talk!" *Oh yeah, it was Elvis: Wise men say/ only fools rush in...*

Wynona Sue opened her front door, looking adorable in a bright red *babydoll negligee, French term for an* <u>*un*</u>*dressing gown that literally means 'neglected'. How tawdry!* Sweet as she was, it was a wonder flies didn't swarm around her head of perfectly coiffed strawberry blonde tresses, *another testament to Orkin hairspray.* That was an endearing sentiment Alex had rehearsed for delivery at the right moment. "You're late, Otto," she said, sticking her head out the door to look up and down the block. "I have roaches crawling out of every crack in the house." *Hmmm? Maybe you should have filled up with vinegar.*

Inside the living room, with the front door shut behind them and all the window curtains closed…"No, no, Honey." *Down girl! You're slobbering on the uniform.* "On advice of counsel—that's the way that mean lawyer you sent me to put it—no whoopee until it's safe. I only came to tell you face to face, and treat your roaches while I'm here." Honey stepped back, crossed her arms across her chest and stomped a foot, *clearly not amused.* "No whoopee?! You haven't come a-courtin' since Sunday. I canceled my Best Little Hair House appointments and exed-out two hours for lunch to be with you, Alex Lehough. Here," she said, stepping forward and grabbing the sleeves of the hazmat suit, "let's get you out of this silly neon-green bug outfit and give Sir Hiss some fresh air." *OMG! Alex, you shared the "pet" nameLouellorene Corker gave to… Do I dare ask what you call this adorable creature in moments of "sheer bliss"?*

"Scarlet, I've decided I would like 'Scarlet' better than 'Ladybug'," Wynona Sue said, yanking at the demron fabric of his disguise. "Henrietta says you remind her of an old fashioned knight who came a-courtin' an Irish princess in one of her college books. His name was Triscuit, but I think Sir Hiss goes better with Scarlet O'Hara, don't you, Sweetie." *Hmmm? Sir Triscuit and Princess Cheezy. What a tasty match.*

Alex managed to free himself. Ladybug, uh, Scarlet, stuck out her lower lip in a adorable pout *Rhett Butler would have LOLed at.* Resisting an almost overpowering urge to embrace and kiss her *which would have been awkward with you in that airless head cage*, he confessed that getting only one D—for desertion— was not quite enough for getting the second D—for divorce from Charlene—and that the legal process was going to be a little more time consuming than he had thought. "Fiddle-de-dee! You promised me a quickie," his passionately impatient fiancee replied, *with unadorably flared nostrils and slitted angry eyes.* "I'm working on it, Honey. Yesterday I got a second mortgage to pay for overtime lawyer work, and while I was up in Okmulgee..." He struggled to get into a pocket sealed with extra-strong velcro.

"Does this little 'hiccup' have anything to do with a certain someone called 'Zander'?" Wynona Sue asked, *in a tone as cold as an iced down keg of beer.* Zander? The question was ridiculous, but his wildly mistaken, possibly even jealous love interest was obviously upset and before he could explain..."Here it is, just for you, uh, Scarlet," he said, holding out a tiny blue...She snatched the tiny blue box out of his hand, *practically bit off its lid like a mongoose decapitating a "Sir Hiss",* and slipped the diamond ring on a finger with a sigh, *like a hangman slipping a noose 'round the neck of a condemned man.* "Well," she said, moving to a window. "Well, I don't know," she said, pulling back curtains to gaze upon the precious gem, *perhaps scratch the little stone across the glass to see if it was really a diamond, and of sufficiently precious carat weight to cut through a protective steel cup Sir Hiss may someday think prudent to wear.*

"Alright, Sir Triscuit," she said, after turning back to him with that adorably pouty lower lip back in place. "As long as I know there's no other...that you are not trifling with me, I suppose tomorrow is another day I can wait for you to make an honest woman of me."

"Well, my dear, it might take a little longer than a day." *I'll say!*

"Now get out of here, Alex. I need to get back to the beauty parlor to show the other girls."

"No, no, please, uh, Scarlet, don't tell a soul, not until the coast is clear. If Charlene found out about our marital plans, well, she might get upset *boil and bubble* and make trouble."

On the way back to his Division Street bungalow, Alex tried to not think too unkindly of Charlene. It was simply his misfortune, and hers, that she had chosen—probably at random—"Shifty" Mashburn to represent her in their divorce. Now both of them seemed to be caught in the cogs of a machine operating independently of any regard for the well being *of anyone but the beastly machine itself.* Finally arriving home, he managed to get out of the hazmat disguise. Feeling exhausted, he collapsed onto the living room sofa. Immediately, he drifted off into a nightmare: *He, sitting naked on the sofa inside Wynona Sue's modest little house. She, wearing a scarlet hazmat suit, drunkenly staggering toward him with a heavy metal box in her arms. "Guess what I've fixed for dinner?" she said, lifting the lid of the box. Strangely terrified by the thought of seeing that Zander had a fish's face, he looked inside the box now turned to cardboard. "Cockroaches!" his new wife said. "Fried to a crisp!" How cruel. "And now that we're married, no more whoopee!" No more whoopee? "Not unless and until you get rid of that 'other' woman!"*

KNOCK! KNOCK! KNOCK!

Alex woke up with a start. In a daze, he went to the door. To his surprise, there stood the lawyer, Willis V. Willis, wearing a business suit and *gravy-stained tie*, grinning *and fully shod.* "Mind if I come in?" the country counselor said, having already entered. "Not disturbing any, uh, social occasion, I hope," he said, looking around *like a garage sale bargain shopper.* "Stood outside the door for a minute or two before knocking and thought I might've heard you talkin' to someone." Alex shook his head negatively. "No? Who's in that room down the hall? I definitely hear..." Alex explained that his pet cockroaches were in the bathroom, hissing. "Hissing, you say? Sounds more like kissing to me. What's goin' on here, Professor? I'm your attorney, sworn to client confidentiality, and you can rest easy that I've heard it almost all before, up to now. So tell me straight, are you into one of those French menageries of three? I need to know and, dang it, I deserve to know. We're in the same sinkin' boat!"

"I...I don't know what you're talking about," Alex said. *I do*, said Zander. *Lipstick on your demron collar, not to mention thinning eyebrows, tells the tale on you.*

"Well then, let me tell you straight what I'm talkin' about," Willis V. Willis said, pacing and looking about the living room. "From a source involved in another case, bound by professional ethics not to tell even me the particulars, I hear that you, unlikely as it would seem..." The heavy-set lawyer stepped back and *is looking at you with wide-eyed disbelief* ". . . have lately been butterin' the biscuits of two women, neither one your legal wife!" *He's on to you, Alex.* "In the eyes of a judge, if this...this kind of French behavior comes out in court, you will be seen as the goldern womanizer in our divorce case. Your cheatin' wife will look innocent as Alice in Wonderland, by comparison! So if you want to ever get through this legal thicket, I am tellin' you again, with no ifs, ands or buts: Pull up your pants, zip up your fly, and stop batter-dippin' the corn dog until...well, I'm not sure your French double-dippin' will be completely legal even then, but at least you'll be single."

His plainspoken country lawyer let out a deep breath, turned and went into the kitchen. Alex followed him. "Just between you, me and the lamp post, Professor," he said, "where have you hid the 'pots and pans' the wife and Shifty Mashburn are so het up to get their greedy hands on? You are, as I say, a legal client, privileged to tell me."

"We buried them," Alex confessed. "For cryin' out loud, lead is too dangerous to keep inside a house. So out in the backyard..."

"'We' buried them, you say?" said his sharp-eared attorney, moving to a window and looking out. "Well then, I want you to promise me on pain of death that late tonight you—all by your lonesome—will dig up the allegedly marital assets and bring the lead box to my office by end of the day tomorrow, for safe keeping away from, uh, varmints, or should I say varmettes?"

"Mr. Willis, please, listen to me, I don't care about the 'assets'." *I do! Half of what's yours is half of what's mine, Alex. That's just the way it is, whether you like it or not.* "I will gladly give Charlene her half, plus half of the remaining half of everything, if only you will hurry up and get me out of marital bondage."

"Way too late to smoke the peace pipe, cowboy," Willis said, facing him with a somber look on his face. "Accordin' to the private detective I hired for you, that wife of yours is off the reservation. I say, likely on the warpath."

"I know she's mad, Charlene has a hot temper, but deep down *she's shallow as a divorced pauper's grave.*"

The country lawyer took a red bandana from a jacket pocket, wiped his suddenly sweaty brow and semi-croaked: "What I mainly came over here to tell you, Professor, is that accordin' to my gol-dern stubbornly ethical source, Virgil Carter has got loose from a head hospial down in Texas after gettin'..."

"Why should I care about Virgil Carter getting...?"

"... knocked in the head, apparently while rasslin' for control of a shotgun. Prints on the butt have been identified..."

Whose butt?

"... as those of your very estranged wife, Charlene Lehough..."

Aha! What a surprise.

"... who I now find has a record long as the whanger of a whale. If you'd told me she was a speeder, lackin' liability insurance, and a petty thief—caught red handed stealin' popcorn at Disney World!—and had such a hot temper, I never would've took the case against her."

Alex was floored. The Charlene he knew was strongly anti-gun butt...*probably no flyswatter handy*...whose only "law breaking" had been participation in peaceful protests against the NRA, against racist flowers, against sexist pencils, and, okay, maybe she also threw rocks at that climate change Denier filling the tank *of a Sunday school van for old folks in wheel chairs. Yelled at them and held up a sign saying JESUS RODE A DONKEY!*

"Well, here's what we gotta do to protect ourselves," Willis V. Willis said, reaching into a jacket pocket, then handing to him... "Your Last Will and Testament, Professor, providing for payment of my fees for time spent gettin' you divorced up to any untimely event of your death, plus appointin' me Executor of your estate. Pro Bono, which means no extra charge for printing."

Alex thanked his generous country lawyer. Willis V. Willis went to a living room window, peeked out, then turned back around. "Get your John Henry notarized on the Will and bring it to my office by end of the day tomorrow." Then, over his shoulder as he bolted toward the door, "And be sure to bring along that box of 'pot and pans', if you want me to keep on tryin' to get you out of holy wedlock before the wife takes matters into her own hands."

As always, determined to get in the last word: *There goes just an honorable country lawyer,* Zander said, *dedicated to making sure every man and woman in the county get his and her day in court, whether they want it or not.*

Twenty-One

Right before start of class, Henrietta's phone buzzed. It was her mother, calling for the third time in the past ten minutes. She took the call, but told Wynona Sue to make it fast. "Operation Bug Spray aborted," her mother said in a hushed tone of voice. "But Operation Roach Trap is a go! Meet at usual place after work for Top Secret report." For cryin' out loud, her mother—though obviously talking in code—made catching Professor Lehough in wedlock sound like a sneaky *Raid* attack on a household pest.

Professor LeRoy:

Dean Rottweiler has advised me that many of you are carrying heavy course loads while also engaged in multiple extracurricular activities, which is why I assigned only a page of reading for todays's class about the famous romantic novel, Wuthering Heights by Emily Bronte. To set the scene for the selected passage...

Agnetta Hurley:

Sorry, Professor, I had to spend all day yesterday and last night in the Emergency Room, being treated for multiple micro aggressions. So I was not psycho able to read the page. Someone wrote "TRUMP" on a blackboard in white chalk!

Barbara Jean Booker:

Get a grip. I am monitoring three graduate school courses in the Victimhood Department. Talk about traumatic!

Charlie Morrison:

I pissed on the shoes of a girl who blew me off and got sent to counseling, so my brain is also blank.

Professor LeRoy:

Anger Management counseling, Charlie? Or dare I ask?

Charlie Morrison:

Building Self Esteem. I may switch my major from Play Station.

Professor LeRoy:

Briefly, I shall synopsize the first half of Wuthering Heights, the classic love story of Catherine Earnshaw and her demonic lover, Heathcliff, to-wit:

She, a minor heiress, and he, a wretched foundling, grew up together on a gloomy manor in desolate moorlands. Both were wild as raw nature itself. They fell in love. But then Cathy became taken by the genteel lifestyle of a neighboring Linton family, and agreed to marry the young family scion, Edgar Linton. To a housemaid, Nelly Dean, (with Heathcliff secretly eavesdropping), she delivered the famous, often quoted, some would say trite, anguished monologue that virtually defines romantic love, absent which no introductory course on the classic love story would be complete, to-wit:

"This is nothing (having told about a dream) I was only going to say that heaven did not seem to be my home; and I broke my heart with weeping to come back to earth; and the angels were so angry that they flung me out into the middle of the heath of Wuthering Heights; where I woke sobbing for joy. That will do to explain my secret, as well as the other. I've no more business to marry Edgar Linton than I have to be in heaven; and if that wicked man in there (her lordly brother) had not brought Heathcliff so low, I shouldn't have thought of it. It

would degrade me to marry Heathcliff now (Heathcliffe goes away mad) so he shall never know how I love him; and that, not because he's handsome (he is a brooding beast) but because he's more myself than I am. Whatever our souls are made of, his and mine are the same.

I cannot express it, but surely everybody has a notion that there is or should be an existence of yours beyond you...I am Heathcliff! He's always, always in my mind: not as a pleasure, any more than I am always a pleasure to myself, but as my own being."

Cathy married Linton, delivered a baby girl not named Joy, and died.

Any questions? Comments?

Agnetta Hurley:

She became a snob, and married for money. I'll bet Edgar Linton was a dentist.

Barbara Jean Booker:

She was a "Beauty" and he was a Beast. This version sounds not as realistic as the movie.

Charlie Morrison:

Is this stuff going to be on the final exam? Not!

Professor LeRoy:

The story has been a subject of endless scholarly analysis and interpretation. Often lost, in my view, is Cathy's motivation. She married Linton, domesticating herself, in hopes of also domesticating Heathcliff. Never a good idea in any level of love story. Psyche, the soul, is by nature no less a wild thing than is Eros. Its domestication is death. Kill the soul, end of love story. Think back to the Othello tragedy. Desdemona dying words might just as well have been those of Cathy if asked who caused her death, to-wit: "I myself."

Henryetta closed her laptop, more than usually confused about why marriage was called a metaphor for happy ending, and semi-fretful about how hard Wynona Sue was trying to "domesticate" Professor Lehough.

Twenty-Two

Back in the burka, back on a bus headed for Okmulgee, back to being herself, Charlene reflected upon her predicament: Without a body, a limb, a finger, a tooth, would the CO2 Gang in Oklahoma City believe she had been murdered? Would they call off their vicious, bloodthirsty dog, Fra Guido? She couldn't be sure she was in the clear of that danger, and now faced another threat. Last night, during precious few pauses in Maximo's unbearably boring commentary on an interminable list of "murrr-derrr cases," she had coaxed the "hardboiled gumshoe" to tell her more about his "Case of a Tramp Named Charlene." Upon hearing that he expected to cross the "butt-swatting dame's" path in a dark alley—and subdue her simply by "showing her his Roscoe"—"Oh my, that sounds dangerous," she'd said sarcastically. But then, with a little more flirtatious coaxing, Max had gone on to reveal "confidential details" of the case indicating real danger, to <u>her</u>! Virgil was back on his feet, likely suffering from lead poisoning of the brain, and probably in deranged, vengeful pursuit of <u>her</u>!

Charlene silently cursed the sexist world into which she had been born. To be free, free, free at last from men, she desperately needed to speed up her divorce from Alex, take the Nobel Prize money she deserved, and make a run for the Mexican border. Standing in her way, she now knew, was not her hopelessly clueless legal husband, not directly, but his male chauvinist legal executioner, Willis V. Willis. According to Maximo, the hard-as-nails divorce lawyer—apparently also a self righteous bible thumper like Swifty—would not be satisfied by anything less than stoning "Charleeene" in public. Getting off the bus in Okmulgee, then walking past the storefront chambers of *Willis V. Willis, Country Lawyer*, Charlene regretted leaving her double-barreled shotgun in the trailer home down on that godforsaken turducken ranch in Texas. With a second blast of buckshot, she would make the world a better place by also removing Thomas "Swifty" Mashburn. A good start, she thought, bringing to mind one of many unfunny lawyer jokes as she pushed open the stained glass door of the hypocritical "parson's" office.

Behind the wire-rimmed lenses perched on his nose, Swifty's eyes brightened. He reached for a button of his vest. "Don't get your hopes up, Swifty," she said, before sitting down across from him. "It's Wednesday and I've got a feeling you haven't done squat to make me unmarried yet. Damnit, you cut me off on Monday, left me on hold for five hours. You ran down my battery; and I neglected to bring a charger when I, uh, relocated from Texas."

"I assure you, Mrs. Lehough, I have been diligently working to make a no longer honest woman of you," the sanctimonious son of a bitch said. "I have labored long and hard in the vineyard of divorce where the grapes of wrath are stored, raking through your husband's financial records with a fine-toothed comb, going at it hammer-and-tong with...Want to know what the V of Willis V. Willis stands for? 'Versus'. And he never fails to live up to it. He's a pathological litigator. Members of the Bar think it's a nickname and say he would sue his own mother simply for the fun of getting her on the stand under cross-examination, but I know better: 'Versus' is his formal name, given to him by his own mother, Aunt Edna. He would more likely sue himself out of spite. Your husband's hired hack is chronically self-conflicted, needlessly stirs up conflict between clients and with the aggrieved spouse's legal representative, in futile quest of his own satisfaction. Willis has tried to bully me since we were boys, living under the same roof..."

" Aunt Edna? You're related to that bastard?"

"Only cousins, but my mother left me in a satchel on her sister's front porch, so we have been in close hand-to-hand conflict with one another since our shared boyhood."

"Seems to me you might have told me this before, Swifty. Seems to me you might have 'conflicted out' of my divorce case."

"Oh no, Willis never refers anyone to me before taking on a client, and vice versa. We have old scores to settle."

"Yeah, well, so do I. Where do we stand, 'Swifty'? You promised to have my divorce settlement done by this coming weekend, remember? That was our deal, and my satisfaction delayed is your satisfaction denied."

"I well remember our deal." *Huff, huff, huff.* "But now I need more on the barrelhead," he said, loosening his bow tie. "So far I haven't yet found conclusive evidence of big prize money hidden in your husband's financial affairs." *Huff, huff, huff.* "If you want me to keep at it..."

"Okay, unbutton your vest and loosen your collar before you choke," she said. "I don't want you to drop dead until after you find that prize money owed to me." Charlene unzipped the burka halfway down to her waist and proceeded to expose her dirty mind: "There once was a girl from Cape Cod/ who thought babies came from God/ But it wasn't the Almighty/ who got under her nightie..."

"You told me that one last week," her sweating lawyer said. "It was Roger the Dodger, by God!" *Huff, huff, huff.* "Tell me another one *huff, huff, huff,* and make it good."

"You drive a hard bargain, Swifty, but okay: One more good one on the barrelhead, but three percent, not five percent on the come."

"Agreed." *Huff, huff, huff.*

"Pat and Mike were at the corner pub, as usual, getting drunk and telling tales of their many sexual conquests, as usual, until Pat's keg ran dry, so to speak. In other words, he couldn't think of any erotic delight except a real one he had experienced years before with his wife, Mary Margaret. 'B'gosh and b'gorra,' he said. 'The happiest time in me life, and I hope it's where I'll be on me dyin' day, was huffin' and puffin' between the milky white thighs of Mary Margaret'."

"Milky white thighs." *Huff, huff, huff.* "Go on, then what?"

"One percent."

"Done. Hurry!" *Huff, huff, huff...*

"Pat stumbled home from the pub, as usual. Mary Margaret, having heard her husband tell his bawdy stories at numerous family gatherings and knowing full well the nature of what he'd been up to, raised a rolling pin above her Irish red-haired head. 'No, not a'tall,' cried Pat, looking into the wife's unsmiling fiery Irish eyes. 'What I told Mike was that the happiest time in me life, and where I hope to end me days was and is, uh, in church with me darlin' Mary Margaret."

"In church. Oh my God!" *Huff, huff, huff...*

"Well, the next day, sure enough, Mary Margaret dropped into Mike's butcher shop to get a raw loin chopped off the bone..."

"Raw loin off the bone." *Huff, huff, huff...*

"...and Mike says to her: 'B'gosh and b'gorra, Mary Margaret, sure and that was a lovely tale Pat told on hisself and you at the pub last night.' To Mike's surprise, Mary Margaret didn't even blush. 'G'on with you, Mike Finegan,' she said. 'Pat's only been there once in the past fifteen years, and even then I had to yank his ear to make him come'."

"Yanked his ear and made him come!" *Huff, huff, huff, huff, huff, huff...*"Would you yank my ear, Mrs. Lehough, in lieu of any percentage of the divorce settlement as my fee, please?"

"No way," Charlene answered, firmly unwilling to stoop to physical degradation even for obtaining her freedom from marriage and safety from brutal men. "But if you don't 'get 'er done' by the weekend, Swifty, I will come back up here and swat your ear with the butt of a shotgun!"

On the sidewalk outside, headed back toward the bus station, Charlene picked up a brick from a stack in front of a building facade under repair. From the middle of the street in front of the next building down, the brick flew from her hand, hit the *V* between *Willis* and *Willis,* shattering the plate glass storefront. Her would-be stoner rushed out of his rustic chambers, barefoot, shaking a fist above his head and shouting...until he saw her... then turned his terrified eyes away and fled up the street like a chicken fearful of being boiled, plucked and stuffed inside a duck inside a turkey.

Twenty-Three

At her *Weekly Herald* desk, Henrietta went about adding a few touches to an article already mostly wrote. Specifically, she started mixing in some quotes she'd got from the story's characters within the past hour. In one place, she typed: *"I had just stepped out of the shower after yoga class," the victim of the alleged assault stated. "I hung my towel on a peg, that then collapsed. That's when I noticed it was a [something else] sticking through a hole."* In another place, she inserted: *"I was in the men's room next door," said the alleged offender. "I thought the hole in the wall was one of those blow machines for drying off after [using a urinal].* Further down in the article, she added: *"I held onto it for fifteen minutes before the police showed up."* There, that made the story about how a couple met last week on Valentine's Day more interesting. Now she could take a break and study up on her next reading assignment, she thought, but...

Police Chief Potter rushed in and hollered, "Stop the presses if it's not too late!" The semi-stocky, semi-middle-aged lawman took his billed cap off a head of mostly black hair recently starting to turn gray in spots, no doubt due to worries about local crime, though in fact there never was any that amounted to much. "Murder!" he said without setting down. "Looks like we may have a case of hot or cold blooded murder on our hands, Henrietta, and a killer on the loose, right here in town!" What in tarnation! Henrietta started typing notes of what Chief Potter went on to read from a sheet of paper he held in a trembling hand: *Postcard with picture of Fountainblue Motel on one side, postmarked Henryetta, OK two days ago, delivered to Boone Oil & Tar Trucking Company in Oklahoma City yesterday. Note from "a friend," handwrote by possibly a child, confessed to murder of a Charlene Leho...*

Henrietta's head jerked up. "Charlene Lehough murdered by a youngun at the Fountainblue Motel?!"

"Not yet confirmed," said Chief Potter, "but stick to your knittin', Henrietta. I want to get this out to the public, then get on over to Professor Lehough's house."

Postcard note indicated killing done "for what she (Charlene Lehough) did to you," indicating likelihood of revenge motive, possibly related to love triangle. Stanley "Biff" Boone, owner of Boone Trucking Company, denied wife's accusation of romantic relationship with the alleged victim; passed nine out of ten lie detector tests and an hour of water-boarding personally administered by Mrs. Boone. No other suspects at this time. Oklahoma City police have referred the matter to local Henryetta, OK law enforcement authorities.

With her stomach balled up and her head feeling semi-offish, Henrietta almost forgot to ask Chief Potter if he had any personal quotes to make the story more interesting. He cleared his throat and she got back to pecking the keyboard: *"All persons are urged to observe extreme caution at all times, especially around children. Anyone who comes across a dead body, regardless of identity—except those of loved ones at licensed funeral homes—should contact local police immediately. Do not, I repeat, do not move the body. Do not, I repeat, do touch any body part whatsoever, unless asked to do so. I have been a police officer for more than twenty years, and was a member of the Kiwanis Club Junior Police in grade school. I have seen more bloody roadkill than I care to remember: Deer, dogs, possums, skunks, armadillos and the like, but never have I heard of anything as grisly as..."*

Henrietta interrupted to suggest to the Chief that maybe he ought to get on over to tell Professor Lehough what might've happened, and leave her to polish up the story. Soon as he left, however, she called Wynona Sue at work. Before she could break it to her mother gently, "Honey, I've got my head in a dryer," she said, "and I've got my own news to tell. Alex dropped by at noon and...Meet me after work at the Ps-n-Qs, as planned."

Henryetta shined up the story—***WOMAN IN SUSPECTED FOUNTAINBLUE FOUL PLAY***—and set to wondering what might have happened. Professor Lehough had been none to happy about Charlene showing up in town with news they were still legally hitched, and Wynona Sue was even less overjoyed by the complication of her romance with the professor. The two of them had squabbled about the matter, and then last Sunday night "Sir Tristan" came a-courtin' with a grocery sack over his head—for heavy sparkin' at the very least—and promised Wynona Sue he was going to get a "quickie" divorce from his wife. Hmmm? Everybody knew endings of happy endings tended to get bitter. In class the other day, Professor LeRoy had got sidetracked into some gloomy sides of classic love stories. The Lehoughs; however, had never seemed involved in a tale that was classic or even semi-romantic. Hmmm?

With Professor Lehough being so noticeably a mild mannered

sort, it was hard to imagine him getting into such a hurried lather to court Wynona Sue without a sack over his head as to fly off his handle and do something foul. And besides, it was the professor his own self—not his wife—who "did" something "to" Oklahoma City oil and tar companies by springing that Lone Star Tick and Alfa Gal tale on them at the climate change trial two years ago. Henrietta her own self had wrote up the story about how surprised and mad the Boones were when their own witness "turned on them" in the witness box.

Hmmm? Maybe someone made up the postcard to put the blame for murder on...who?

Later, at the P's-n-Q's pool hall and quaint cafe, waiting for her mother..."Wynona Sue called to say she's on her way," said a waiter, as he set on the table a tin bucket of ice with the tip of a bottle stickin' out the top. "I already uncorked the champagne." Uh oh, her mother had in mind a party to celebrate a special occasion—Henrietta heard wedding bells chiming—and the news about Charlene Lehough was going to spoil it for her, but... Wynona Sue, with a new behind-her-ears hairdo and blue ribbon on top, got there and set down. Without a word, her mother brought a black-gloved hand from behind her back, held it up, and wiggled a finger. "It's official, Henrietta," she whispered. "As of noonish today I am betroughed to Professor Alexander Lehough." The waiter filled up two wine glasses. The bride to be raised hers and said, "But you can't put the news in the paper 'til next week, or even gossip about it 'til Alex gets past the second 'D'."

"Second 'D'?"

"From that old movie and TV series," said her mother, "*Witches of Eastwick*, one of my all time favorites. 'D' for desertion, then 'D' for divorce from that...well, let's not spoil the mood by even mentioning that...that woman's name in polite company."

Feeling like they were dancing on poor Charlene Lehough's grave, Henrietta broke the news to Wynona Sue gently as she could manage. Off came the glove. "'D' for death!" her mother said, holding up her bare hand decorated with a gold ring that might have had a spec of diamond stuck on it.

"'D' for death!" That was unseemly, even for Wynona Sue.

"Fiddle-dee-dee," said her mother. "That brunette hussy probably wrote the postcard her own self to try to get everyone to feel sorry for her. But frankly, my dear, I don't give a hoot! She can play possum for a change, not me anymore."

Fiddle-dee-dee? Henrietta had never before heard her mother utter the word, or any word so out of place for such a special occasion as that of a suspected murder. Then it hit her: On Monday, the day after she her own self had made a joke about Professor Lehough courtin' Wynona Sue on the sly like a "Sir Tristan," her mother had called her at the office to get the name of the Irish princess the English knight had romanced in the book. "Isolde?" she'd said. "No, I like Scarlet better." Since then, Wynona Sue must have ordered up that old *Gone With the Breeze* movie on a pay-per-view channel. "I am Irish on my daddy's side," she'd added. And had always been inclined to princessness, Henrietta had thought at the time.

"I wouldn't take it so 'fiddle-dee-dee' like, if I was you," she advised her mother, "and I would put that glove back on. Chief Potter went over to the professor's house about an hour ago and is no doubt asking a lot of questions."

"Questions? About what? Great balls of fire, Henrietta, they have been all but legally divorced for years. Alex knows nothing about that...that woman, and doesn't want to know." From the way her mother talked, it suddenly seemed she must have grew up somewhere in the Deep South.

"Maybe so, but someone's been wantin' to know somethin' about 'that woman'," said Henrietta, taking a business card out of her tote. "That chubby fella who used to work in the back room of the post office came by the other day—'Maximo Morgan', it says here on his card, 'Private Detective'—askin' all kinds of questions about Mrs. Lehough."

"Do not ever again use that term in my presence."

"So after Chief Potter came by, I got to thinkin' that maybe... Did the professor ever say anything about hiring a private detective to snoop..."

"Private investigations are strictly confidential, Henrietta, and it's not snooping."

Oh no, from the odd look on her mother's face..."You your own self didn't hire Mr. Maximo to be confidential about anything, I hope."

"Great balls afire, Henrietta, I barely know the man."

"Barely?"

"Alright, if you must know, last week I was gettin' my beautician license renewal forms notarized. I may have mentioned in passing that I was curious, simply curious to know if any post office customers went by the name...not 'Mrs. Anybody!'... possibly a 'Miss, uh, Zander Somebody'."

Unlike Wynona Sue a/k/a Scarlet—who went on to say, "Fiddle-dee-dee, I'll think about it tomorrow"—Henrietta went back to wondering what might have happened to poor Mrs. Lehough. And later, back at her singles-only Shangri-La apartment, went to googling. She discovered that *The Witches of Eastwick* was a book that got made into a movie that got made into a TV series about three middle-aged gals who had been done wrong by men. They were bitter and feeling sorry for theirselves until a stranger came to town and had his way with all three of them. They were lucky, he told them. When a gal got rid of a no-account man by any of "the three D's—desertion, divorce, or death—when that happens, she blossoms. Like flowers. Like fruit. She is ripe. That's the woman for me." Turned out he was the Devil. In the end, the gals got together and with witchcraft tricks they had learned, made him disappear.

Hmmm? Henrietta had a hard time imagining Professor Lehough as devilish, but not such a hard time thinking of Wynona Sue as witchish.

Twenty-Four

Max steered a Lazy Susan ninety degrees clockwise to transport a quart-size pitcher of maple syrup to his place at a kitchen table, then poured half of it onto a six-inch stack of pancakes. Sandy sat next to him, drinking black coffee and smoking a cigarette. His mother stood across the small kitchen at a stove, frying bacon. He unfolded a *Weekly Herald* delivered earlier that Friday morning and with his dripping fork halfway twixt plate and lip...Hel-lo, what was this? ***WOMAN IN SUSPECTED FOUNTAINBLUE FOUL PLAY.*** Quickly he grasped... Murrr-derrr! "Well, that puts D.O.A. on a toe of the tramp named Charlene," he said aloud to himself. "Case closed." Sandy grabbed the newspaper, stared at its front page for a few seconds, then said, "Criminy! Why in hell would the CO2 Gang call the cops? Shit!" His mother jerked her head around, a disapproving frown on her face. Max, accustomed to rough street talk, remained calm. CO2 Gang? "Oil and tar thugs in Oklahoma City," Sandy explained. "They obviously wanted, uh, Charlene dead, as revenge for her well known ardent support of the climate Cause. Someone did them a favor, and this is how the bastards show their gratitude," she said, swatting the *Weekly Herald* with the back of a hand.

She was a babe alright, the kind of semi-sweet young thing that got lost in the woods after failing to leave a trail of cookie crumbs. Time for the kid to learn the facts of life, Max decided. "Sorry to ruin your conspiracy theory, Sweetheart," he said. "Charlene Lehough is likely only the victim of a love affair gone foul." Sandy's big round eyes told all: The kid was clueless about the kinds of things that went on between guys and dolls caught up in fits of passion. "Remember that grifter by the name of Virgil Carrr-terrr I put you wise to, the joker who had a beef with a dame down in Texas? Yeah, she was a blonde, they say, but the way things have turned out, the turducken ranch broad must have been Charleeene wearing a wig. When Carter skipped out of that Domino, Texas hospital Sunday night, with a splitting headache you might say, he was no doubt in a mood for revenge against the deadly dame who put him there." Sandy's eyes got even bigger and rounder. "Just like a man to blame Charlene for what that son of a bitch had coming!" she said.

The babe's feminine instinct to shift blame was probably right on the money, Max thought, while mopping up his syrupy plate with remains of the last pancake. Probably Carrrt-errr was a heeel who..."It's your fault, Max," said Sandy. "You let the son of a bitch slip past you, and find Charlene before you did. Now you're going to sit on your big be-hind and let that professor take her pot of gold, even though he was the true climate change Denier who screwed over the Boones and let Charlene and Virgil take the fall. And I thought you were almost as sharp a shamus as Jessica Fletcher. Boy, was I wrong!" Max remained calm, but pushed his chair back from the table, slightly. His appetite was gone, almost. "Sandy's right," said his mother, snatching a plate of blueberry muffins off the Lazy Susan. "Jessica never would have allowed such foul shit to happen right under her nose!" Two to one; only a sucker would play gotcha against those odds. The hard, cold facts of life were that he—not unlike Mike Hammer in the *Case of Kiss me, Deadly*—may have made a mistake that might have cost a dame her life. Like Mike, determined to put things right, Max mentally re-opened the *Case of a Tramp Named Charlene.*

Fifteen minutes later, he ankled into the local police station, tossed his business card onto a desk tended to by a uniformed flatfoot. "Whatta we got, Pat?" he asked. "Pat who?" said the copper. "My name's Pete Potter." Max apologized for the slip of tongue—Captain Pat Chambers was the New York police homicide honcho Mike Hammer regularly solved crimes for—but with a killer on the loose, dispensed with further professional courtesies and got down to brass tacks: "Any sign of Virgil Carrr-terrr?" he asked the small town Barney Fife.

"Virgil Carter? You mean the guy who ran for County Commissioner and Vice-President? We took down all his signs years ago." Potter was obviously a farm team player, nowhere near ready for the big league.

"I mean the Virgil Carter who blew town two years ago with a certain bruuunette Molly, namely Charleeene Lee-hooough."

The desk jockey, still ignoring the business card on the desk, fish-eyed him up and down. "Who are you?" he asked.

"The Fat Mannn," Max growled. "Two-hundred forty-odd pounds. Fortune: Dangerrr."

"Oh yeah, you're the guy who used to work at the post office. I didn't recognize you in that hat and suit and...Where'd you get those shoes?"

"Private dicking is my lay these days."

The small town Five-O took off his cap and scratched his bean, obviously impressed. "Yeah," he said, "you could be onto something. I gotta admit: I never thought of Virgil Carter as a suspect in...It's not a murder case, at least not yet. No dead body has turned up. Professor Lehough says he saw his wife late last week, alive and well."

"Forget Lehough. Carter likely skated Texas Sunday night, the postcard copping to his moll's murder was posted from here on Monday of this week and...Let me guess: Charlene Lehough's alive and well body has not shown up eeeither, right?"

"No, not yet," Chambers, uh, Potter admitted, with his head down, finally eyeballing the business card. "'Maximo Morgan, Private Detective'," he mumbled, before looking up with squinted eyes.

"Haven't turned pro yet," Max admitted. "But you can take it to the bank from yours truly, Brad Run...The Fat Mannn is no amateurrre at the whooodunnit gammme."

"Great," Pat Potter agreed. "To tell the truth, Maximo, in my own long career in law enforcement, I have run across more roadkill than I care to remember: Deer, dogs, raccoons, but...all of those dead bodies were easy to find on the highway. Where should I look for, uh, Mrs. Lehough's, uh, remains?"

"Have you drained the lake yet?" One of the first things he'd learned from Mike: Water was thicker than aiiir. H2O was not a healthy bev-errr-age except for merrr-maaaids.

"Lake Henryetta? That's the town reservoir, with more than ten miles of shoreline, over four-hundred surface acres of drinking water."

"Dredge every square inch of it," Max advised. "Get back to me with what you find. I'll take care of the Fountainblue Motel swimming pooool," he added, before heeling-and-toeing out of the police station.

An old guy at the Fountainblue check-in counter, bald as a billiard ball, identified himself as owner of the in-town resort motel. In answer to Max's question, "We don't have a swimmin' pool no more," he claimed. Hmmm? A dead end. Max put a light green refresher on the counter. "By any chance, do you happen to recall a recent guest named Virgil Carrr-terrr—wears specs, big nose, black mustache—who would have checked in late Sunday night or Monday?" The old guy glanced at a pad of paper also lying on the counter and shook his hairless head sideways. Another dead end. Another light green refresher. "But I think we might've had that gal stay with us for a few nights recently, the one they say maybe got murdered."

Bingo!

"Name of Charlene Lehough? Five to six feet in height, brunette broad?"

"Couldn't say for sure. Signed in as 'Jane Doe' apparently, and I never got a good look at her my own self. Just reports from my boy, Hughie, mainly about dirty jokes she told him."

Jane Doe? The name rang a bell, but..."Hughie's gone off to Cancun, Mexico for what they call 'Spring Break'," the cue ball said, "even though it's not even March yet. That's why I did some lookin' around Room Twelve and later happened to start thinkin' 'Jane Doe' might be the real name of the gal who probably got murdered."

"Oh yeah? What tipped you off?"

"She must've been the one who stole the postcard, I figured. Dang it, the picture on it was for decor, and we've only got a few of 'em left to remind folks of back when the Fountainblue was just like somethin' you'd see on Miami Beach, Florida. That dirty minded gal, she was no angel, that's for sure."

"Yeah, I doubt plunking a golden harp is her lay these days. If I were you, oldtimer, I would check all the other roooms and..."

"Don't worry, I already checked 'em but..."

"...pick up any other picture postcards layin' around."

"...found no woman's dead body, just a skunk."

Max backed out of the deluxe dead end, ankled to his mother's parked car, sat at the wheel and tried to dope out what Brad Runyon's next move would be. The *Case of a Tramp Named Charlene* had become a tangled bowl of spa-ghet-ti and...With angel hair pasta parmigiana in mind, Max decided to drift over to the Chair Crushers Cafe for a mid-morning snack. Maybe with a little nourishment, his brain—that he sometimes thought of as a hamster inside his head—would sniff out something he'd missed.

Driving his mother's old Buick toward the west edge of town, he couldn't shake a gnawing sense that the case against Virgil Carter was lame as a faux crab salad. Carter himself had not checked into the Fountainblue. How would the dark-haired pots and pans salesman—with a lead plate lodged in his head—have had the moxie to track Charlene Lehough to Room Twelve of the motel? Yeah, dollar to a do-nut, she was there alright, under the name Jane Doe. Hmmm? Jane Doe... Jane Doe...Jane Dough... No, nothing came to him except images of a pizza spinning in air. Max arrived at the Chair Crushers joint with nothing to bait the hamster. Fifteen minutes later, however, right on cue with with his first forkful of angel hair, the sharp-nosed rodent inside him began to sniff at something possibly foul. The wheel inside his head began to turn and turn and turn and...From somewhere a marble rolled into a slot numbered 1524, as in 1524 Division Street, residence of Professor Alexander Lehough!

Could be the floozie he'd overheard playing kissy-kissy-kissy with Lehough in his bathroom was not the mysterious dame called Zannn-derrr. Could be the promiscuous professor was engaged in attempted make-up s-e-x with his recently returned wife. Days later they were living together again, so to speak, in Splitsville, a town known for its high rate of assault, battery and murrr-derrr. Hmmm? But Professor Lehough was technically still his client once removed through Willis Willis. Investigation of him in connection with the disappearance of Charlene Lehough might be professionally unethical. And jeopardize his pending application for a P.I. ticket. No, Lehough was clean. Sandy's naive suspicions about the professor setting up Charlene and Carter now sounded crazy as the paranoid ravings a guy might hear out of the kisser of a an adulterous wife fearful of a betrayed husband's revennnge.

The *Case of Fatal Attraction* came to mind, but...Something about a dame boiling a pet rabbit...alive...Hmmm? Max couldn't get a handle on why the hamster had spun that one to him. Maybe just an expression of varmint sol-id-arity. As he twisted onto his fork tresses of blonde angel hair—tinged with strawberry-red traces of tomato sauce—his ex-client in the *Case of a Vamp Called Zander* next came to mind. Yeah, maybe the strawberry blonde knock-out found out her fiance was back to playing hide the cannoli with his legal wife. Now that Max thought about it, the postcard sent to the oil and tar couple in Oklahoma City by the killer—claiming he...or she... did the deadly deed "for you"—reeked of a certain cheap perfuuume known as *Eau de Femme Fatale.*

Max mentally opened a new *Case of The Jealous Strawberry Blonde*, about a delectable little dish named Wyyynona Suuue.

Twenty-Five

Standing at the *Weekly Herald* storefront window, looking out at the main street of her little ol' hometown, Henrietta took stock: Five years ago, after dropping out of Murray State when it was a junior college, she had started off her career as Classified Ad Editor for the Paris Flea Market Section of the paper. Then, as Sports Editor responsible for writing down scores of local school games, she broke the story of illegal recruiting of high school boys—in particular Gaylord Goodhart—to play bigtime prison football that had replaced bigtime college football. As Editor-at-Large, assigned to digging up hard news, she was first to report on Virgil Carter's campaign for County Commissioner as a Democrat that led to his nomination for Vice-President of the United States. Promoted up to being Assistant Editor-in-Chief, she led investigation of the big viral story—***GRIM REAPER GETS OUT OF DODGE!***—that turned out to be the Mayor's mistake about the miracle powers of local water. But dang it, then her article about the "climate trial" that *The New York Times* printed had a dern typo in it. Her dream had always been to get noticed in a good way, get a job at a big city newspaper, and someday win one of those Pulitzer Prizes for telling important news.

Now, there she was, smack dab on the spot of a whodunnit that might be her last chance to make a name for her own self. If Charlene Lehough got murdered—like the note someone wrote and her missing condition made likely—an investigative reporter who got to the bottom of the mystery might get a big break, she reckoned. Hmmm? Henrietta had a suspicious notion that Butch Bernard and Roy Potter—who seemed to care more about making metal robots more humanlike than being humanlike their own selves to actual living creatures—might have chopped up poor Mrs. Lehough for bones and skin needed to carry on with their export business, but...She went to her desk and picked up her buzzing eye-phone. Chief Potter was calling.

"Henrietta, this is not to be put in the paper, at least not yet," he said, "but it looks like Virgil Carter likely murdered Mrs. Lehough." What in tarnation?! The Chief went on to explain that according to a private detective named Maximo Morgan the likely victim, Charlene Lehough, had fetched the butt of a shotgun upside Virgil Carter's head down in Texas only six days before the note got sent from the Fountainblue Motel. And only one day before the murder, Virgil had busted out of a hospital with a lead plate stuck in his head, no doubt mad as a rained on rooster. "Gotta go," Chief Potter then said. "No time to chat, not with a killer on the loose." Hmmm? Both Virgil and Charlene were on the side of the farmers and ranchers in that climate trial; Virgil was supposed to have been the star witness against the Boone group; and she her own self had seen the two of them at the courthouse, getting hitched, she'd thought, by one of those cloaked monks. Though Virgil and Charlene never got legally married, they likely had a Mr.-and-Mrs. type spat, she reckoned, and probably he chased her to town and committed foul play.

Dang it, mate murders were common as pig tracks; not the makings of a big story unless someone famous was involved, as in the case of the King and Queen of England in a movie re-run she watched on TV last year. Hmmm? Now that she thought about it, Professor Lehough was in about the same fix as that eighth King Henry—in a lather to get a divorce so he could marry another gal—and according to what she had learned in college, famous old stories such as that one tended to repeat theirselves. But would Professor Lehough go so far as to chop off his wife's head? Wynona Sue might do it, but…Heck, either way, no one except folks in town would likely take much notice of such a tale.

Hmmm? ***HATCHET MEN HARVEST HEAD AND HANDS FOR A HER!*** would be a big story alright, but the route to such an investigative report was just too dern scary. On the other hand, Henrietta reckoned there was about nothing she wouldn't do to get a big city newspaper job and maybe win one of those Pulitzer Prizes.

According to Mr. Harold, her getting a liberal arts college education would be useful to her understanding what went on in the world she lived in, and to understanding her own mind. But today was the final class in the course about the classic love story of passion, jealousy and hate and she doubted she would learn anything helpful to figuring out a whodunnit mystery.

Professor LeRoy:

The Phantom of the Opera originated as a serialized novel written by Gaston LeRoux in 1909, supposedly inspired by historical events. The classic story was adapted for the musical stage by Andrew Lloyd Webber in 1986, and later got made into a musical movie based on the play. I much prefer the stage version for being more mystical, more magical, more moving. In case any of you had time to only scan SparkNotes, perhaps watch a few YouTube segments, I shall briefly summarize, to-wit:

The story begins with an old man, Raoul, attending an auction of artifacts from the long gone Paris Opera House, notably including an enormous chandelier that has been repaired. The auctioneer says that some in attendance may recall "the strange affair of the Phantom of the Opera, a mystery never fully explained." Magically, the chandelier "becomes illuminating" and rises to the ceiling, taking Raoul back to when he was young and the Paris Opera House was in its prime. Then and there he again meets an aspiring prima donna of sixteen or perhaps seventeen years of age, Christine. She retires to a dressing room and tells another female performer that her recently magnificent singing was inspired by an "Angel of Music" in a dream. Later, she will further explain that in her dream she was enveloped in swirling mist rising from a vast glassy lake. There were lighted candles all around. On the lake was a boat, and in the boat there was a man.

Does that sound like the beginning of a "mystery," or could anyone foresee what was bound to happen?

Charlie Morrison:

Yeah, I bought the flick and foreseen clear as day. The auction number for the light fixture was six-six-six. Dude in the boat was the Devil.

Barbara Jean Booker:

Hmmm? I'll take a wild guess and say what's bound to happen is another classic love story.

Agnetta Hurley:

Spoiler alert!

Professor LeRoy:

Specifically, what next happens is that we hear a loud, angry, jealous voice—which proves to be that of the half-masked Phantom—then Christine sees him in her dressing room mirror, steps through it and follows him into his lair under the opera house. They join in a strange haunting duet, in which the Phantom rather jealously takes credit for Christine's performances, and she concedes that she is "the mask" he wears, it's him people hear when she sings. Again she refers to her dream, singing that now she finds "the Phantom of the Opera is there, inside her mind." Later the Phantom will more jealously complain that it is her singing that made Raoul fall in love with her. Yes, Raul and Christine become lovers, he gives her a ring, which she insists on wearing on a chain around her neck to keep their engagement secret. Theirs is a love story, but is it "classic"? Similarly, when the Phantom jealously wreaks murder and mayhem inside and to the opera house, there is no "mystery" to his actions. No whodunnit plot to figure out.

No, the mystery is that Christine, though fearful for her life, has fallen in love with the Phantom. When the chandelier crashes to the floor. He abducts her from the opera house that has caught fire and again takes her to his subterranean lair. He gives her the ring that he had snatched from her chain and asks her to stay with him. Raoul follows, to rescue her, but is trapped by the Phantom. Christine, confronted with a fateful choice, puts the ring on her finger, takes the mask from the Phantom's grotesquely disfigured face, and kisses him passionately. Raoul knows then that she loves the Phantom. More importantly, the Phantom also understands that profound truth, but also accepts that Christine must live her life in the outside world, where he cannot be openly with her. So he lets her and Raoul go. As an angry mob from the outside world crashes into his lair, well, I much prefer the stage play ending in which the Phantom wraps himself in his dark cloak and disappears.

So, as a kind of warm up for next week's final exam, query: Who or what was the Phantom and what happened to him?

Charlie Morrison:

Like I said at the git go, he was and still is the Devil. I go up against him all the time on Play Station, but the sumbitch keeps coming back.

Barbara Jean Booker:

What he was is simple: A creepy music teacher. He should end up in jail.

Agnetta Hurley:

Trigger! Trigger! Trigger! It's a story about a professor hitting on a female student! Call Dean Rottweiler!

Professor LeRoy:

What do you say, Henrietta? Who or what was the Phantom and what happened to him? Come on, anyone who has been as quiet and attentive in my course as you should know the answer.

Henrietta, for some reason back to thinking about Professor Lehough—as a King of England dissatisfied with a wife named Queen Ann—was caught off guard by the question put to her. Hmmm? She had bought the DVD movie version of the *Phantom* tale on Amazon for two-dollars and ninety-eight cents. Twice she had watched it through to the end, to when Mr. Raoul went back to the time of being old and paid a visit to Christine's grave. The Phantom's black ribbon was laying there and on top of it the ring Christine had put on her finger years before. Hmmm? Henrietta typed: *Well, he was a phantom, sort of like a ghost, so I reckon…*

Professor Le Roy:

Right! The Phantom was Christine's animus, her inner masculine self, her soul that escaped her earthly body forty-seven years after the "mystery never fully explained," until now.

Charlie Morrison:

Let's give Professor LeRoy the clap.

Professor LeRoy:

Thank you one and...one, Charlie. In conclusion of this course on the classic love story, a tale of passion, jealousy and hate, I leave you with this—a conundrum, if you will—for you to chew on as you attempt to find "usefulness" of your liberal arts education: On the one hand, the brilliant Carl Jung recognized that the real life experience of falling in love was projection of one's soul image onto another. On the other hand, Dr. Jung saw the very purpose of life as achievement of what he termed "individuation," the regaining of a lost sense of wholeness that can can only occur when one reclaims and absorbs into himself or herself those very projections. Understanding the drama that takes place inside our minds as manifest in the classic love story can be helpful to the process. In other words, Henrietta: It is you who are the seeker, and it is you are the sought. This is the divine romance.

Final exam will be posted next Thursday, and I am sure at least one of you will do well.

The others in class started yelling *TEACHER'S PET! TEACHER'S PET! HENRIETTA IS THE TEACHERS PET!* along with some other things about her even more uncomplimentary. So without giving Professor LeRoy "the clap," Henrietta shut down her laptop. Hmmm? For some reason—maybe her liberal arts education taking hold—she had a funny feeling she had finally got over Gaylord Goodhart.

Twenty-Six

Alex tried to focus his mind on what mattered—his very interesting analysis of the boll weevil that he had already titled *Pest or Panacea?*—not on unfounded speculation about Charlene possibly *based on nothing more than her own prank postcard from hell.* If only the boll weevil's appetite for cotton buds and flowers could be redirected to chemical fibers *like the chicken farming industry has so successfully done with human children* otherwise noxious waste could be recycled. He tried humming an old song: *Boll Weevil said to the farmer/ We gotta have a home/ Lookin' for a home/ Gotta have a home*...but that didn't work. Alex got up from the desk in his study, mentally paralyzed by a sense of...of guilt *for what now? Wearing cotton socks and taking food out of the mouths of a weevil family?* Once upon a time, Charlene and he had been in love, perhaps not madly *but at least as crazy as two waltzing mice* and now she might be... gone forever. *Each man kills the thing he loves, said the poetically inclined condemned man. Don't be so hard on yourself, Alex.*

"No man is an island," he responded in kind, "every man is a piece of continent. If a clod be washed away by sea, the homeland is made less." *In this case, I see love and life as a zero sum game: Loss of a certain clod from somewhere, per the natural process of avulsion, is our island's gain of silt*.

"Anyone's death diminishes me. And if I were you, Zander, I would be asking for whom the bells toll." *Point taken: All love is self love; all mourning is for one's self; all pity is self pity; all guilt a version of what the shrinks call schadenfreunde: Funereal glee that it is someone other than ourselves who has circled the drain.*

"Well, how could I not feel guilty?" Alex muttered. "That policeman who delivered the news seemed to think I had something to do with...with whatever happened to Charlene." *Spouses are always suspects numero uno, which says something about the marital bliss you're so hot to re-enjoy with another, wouldn't you say?* "My marital intentions regarding Wynona Sue have nothing to do with...with whatever happened to Charlene." *Except provide a specific motive for murder.* Murder?! "We had already, uh, have already agreed to divorce," *which might have taken years, during which time another froggie might have come a-courtin your ladylove: Scarlet now, right?* Alex picked up his phone and punched in Willis Willis' number. *Good idea. Don't say anything more to that cop except through a legal mouthpiece.*

"Professor Lehough, my favorite client," said the twangy voice of his country divorce attorney. "I was just now fixin' to call you with good news: You're in the clear." Clear, meaning single again? "Accordin' to my multiple sources down there at the scene of the crime, there is another suspect numero uno and, well, no need to go into that. The point is that we soon might be rid of that pesky sumbitch, Shifty Mashburn." Single again? "Well, in due time, Professor, in due time." *Uh oh, or should I say cha-ching!* "My personal opinion is that your wife is not yet dead, but more likely caged-up down there at Gitmo. And that's a relief to yours truly, I can tell you."

Alex, stunned—even Zander was speechless—could only listen in disbelief as the country lawyer from Okmulgee went on to say that Charlene, always ardent about a multitude of causes—had become a radical Islamic terrorist! "When she first came in to see me—wearin' one of those all-black A-rab outfits—well, you never can tell what a gal will put on her back. My wife had already told me black was the new orange in women's clothes and I didn't want to get my ass sued for bein' what they call politically uncorrect. But when she came back the other day and threw a bomb through my window..."

"A bomb?!" *A bomb?!*

"Thankfully, it was a dud. Fella from the police bomb squad put it in a box but still can't get 'er to go off."

Alex was incredulous. *I don't know why. Her favorite pastime was to shout DEATH TO DENIERS! DEATH TO GUN OWNERS! DEATH TO CARNIVORES! DEATH TO JESUS! On the other hand, I have to admit DEATH TO LAWYERS has a certain happy ring to it.*

"Of course the Feds will never admit what they've done or will do to her. So you and me, podner, are caught like two cattle rustlers in a snapped-off, rolled-up coil of barb wire. We could go ahead and try to divorce the wife in absentia on grounds of abandonment for a period of at least a year, unless, uh, there just might be a certain someone out there who might pop up out of stump and say he'd seen or overheard, uh, recent sexual congress between you two, which would re-start the clock. We can't prove imprisonment or even conviction of a felony as grounds, seein' as how the Feds are so stubborn about not playin' along with due process of law. And so far, we've not actually caught your wife in the company of another man with her knickers down, so adultery is not yet provable."

"What about death? What if they find…a body?" *You're just sayin', right?*

"That's is somethin' you should <u>not</u> be sayin' to no one, Professor, not even to your privileged lawyer. At least not 'til a decent interval passes by, for appearances' sake if nothin' else."

"Decent interval? You said that a spouse's death was the quickest D to a man's freedom from an unhappy marriage." *Alex, shut up!*

"That was the Devil talkin' in a gol-dern movie, not yours truly! And neither one of us ever promised quicker. If you ever claim I put you up to somethin', well, the first thing I'm gonna do is unweld this lead box you hauled over here, sealed up tighter than a mule's anus in fly season. Then I'm gonna…"

"The box is steel, the pots and pans are made of lead! Do not open the box!"

"Well, if that's your story, stick to it, if asked. The Devil was semi-truthful, as usual—in event of your wife's death, the divorce case will be done with, you'll be single—but then, well, you might say there's still the Devil's due to pay."

"Single, that's all I ever wanted. I will happily pay the Devil." *Alex, what have you done?*

"That's good to know, 'cause If Shifty Mashburn got your wife to make him executor of her estate, well, we could find ourselves back in a different court up against him. And even then…"

"I don't care about any estate. I just want to go on with my life at any cost."

"You're startin' to make me nervous, Lehough, so let me give it to you straight. In the unlucky event your wife shows up alive, or luckily dead for that matter, until we've pissed on the campfire and called in the dogs, I strongly recommend that you cool off your brandin' iron and put it back in the saddle bag. What I mean plain and simple is stay clear of any, say, strawberry blonde heifer who might happen to cross your path. I will leave it at that."

Lucky event? Unlucky event? *Well, they say you can't kill a vampire.* Stay clear of Wynona Sue? *Seems like the sensible thing to do, under the regrettable circumstances and all.* Alex hung up on Willis V. Willis, once and for all. *How did he know about your discreet romantic forays, Sir Triscuit?* What nonsense, and with Charlene not even *risen from a grave to haunt us.*

Feeling guilty and ashamed for ever even thinking about wanting *to simply be "rid of" the wife,* Alex rummaged through a desk drawer. At the bottom of assorted bits of memorabilia he found a twenty-year-old photo of *OMG, is that half of you on the cropped edge?* In the foreground: Charlene, his student at the time, *still brandishing that FREE WILLY! placard two years after the celebrity whale escaped from SeaWorld and swam into the wild.* In the background: A movie theatre marquee—*Free Willy II; Adventure Home*—took his mind back to the protest march they led, not really to free Willy, per se—*who had died within a year of his homecoming in the real-life sequel*—but to *SAVE THE BARNACLES!* attached to whales, *lookin' for a home, but in danger of going down with the ship, so to speak.* Charlene was so young back in 1995, so naive, so idealistic, *so already pissed off at the world back then,* he recalled, as a tear ran down his cheek and dropped off the tip of his walrus mustache onto perhaps his last remaining image of *the barnacle who later attached herself to your backside.*

Feeling guiltier, *perhaps about not feeling guiltier?* Alex picked up his phone and placed a call. Before his obviously excited fiancee could tempt him, he said, "Wynona Sue, we need to talk." *About more than just appearances of pitching woo with a brown paper sack over your head, looking, uh, guilty of something.*

Twenty-Seven

Arriving at her singles-only Shangri-La apartment on Friday evening, Henrietta was alarmed to see Butch Bernard setting on a flower pot outside the front door, holding a flashlight and looking at the front page of that week's paper headlined ***WOMAN IN SUSPECTED FOUNTAINBLUE FOUL PLAY***. He was grinning like a frog who had just caught a fly with his sticky tongue, even before looking up and grinning wider at the sight of her. "Hey, Henrietta," he said. "I was at that pool hall waitin'; saw you come in and then turn around; so I walked over here to catch you." Catch her? She had spotted him inside the P's-n-Q's and decided to go by Cox Liquors and bring home a six-pack of beer. "I came prepared," he said searching a shirt pocket stuffed with pens. "Look," he said, holding up his eye dropper. "Let's party. Yuk, yuk, yuk."

She told him she wasn't in the mood to have a good time; just wanted to relax and watch TV. He stuck a hand into a pants pocket and whipped out... a DVD. "Then let's get right to it," he said. "You need to watch *Ex Machina* at least once—with me explaining—if you wanna be a member of the... Me and Roy changed our team name to *Skin & Bone Soul Mates.* Ain't that sexy. Yuk, yuk, yuk." The odor of his aftershave cologne was downright sickening.

Inside her apartment, she went into the kitchenette and looked in a drawer, but didn't find anything sharp she could put in a jeans pocket. Without opening a can of beer, she went back to the living room, where Butch was putting *Ex Machina* into the DVD player, but talking about the other movie on the subject of an artificially intelligent "soul mate" titled *Her.* "Samantha was just an AI OS," he said, "and someone wrote that she 'made men able to experience love and affection beyond physical into virtual', but..." He turned to her, bright out of the eyes behind his coke bottle bottoms. "Roy has done it all virtually," he said. "He had a date with Taylor Swift, naked, and said that she wasn't so hot. Yuk, yuk, yuk. Now he knows that only a metal, I mean skin and bone soul mate can do the trick." Butch set on the divan. She set on the edge of a chair, wondering if there were any remains of poor Mrs. Lehough's skinless and boneless body that would ever turn up, in the United States.

Henrietta semi-watched and semi-listened to the movie as Butch explained what was happening on the TV screen. A young fella named Caleb arrived somewhere by helicopter and met an older fella named Nathan, who told Caleb he had been picked to take a "Turing Test" to see if he could resist believing that an artificially intelligent humanoid named Ava was a real woman. "The names are from the Bible book," Butch said. "'Ava' is a form of 'Eve', the first human woman, though later you will see a de-commissioned prior model who was named 'Lily' for some reason. 'Caleb' was a spy sent by someone called Moses to check out a place called the Promised Land. And Nathan was a prophet, which means he could see into the future." Ava came into the picture, with a cute human face and regular hands and feet, but with a steel cap instead of hair and a metal, though shapely robot body. Sure enough: She proved to be wily as Eve her own self. Henrietta paid attention.

Somehow Ava knew how to shut off power so that Nathan couldn't watch Caleb and her with cameras while she flirted and obviously got Caleb to fall in love with her. She warned him not to trust Nathan. Without necessarily thinking of *Ex Machina* as a classic love story—due to all the jabber between Caleb and Nathan, who seemed to always be drunk—Henrietta got to feeling like she was in one of Professor LeRoy's classes. The gist of their conversations seemed to be about whether or not Nathan had specifically programmed Ava to be Caleb's "type of gal"—maybe by hacking into his computer "pornography profile," Caleb suspected—which would have amounted to cheating on the Turing Test. Nathan denied it and started talking about a famous painter who created art without thinking. The challenge, he said was to create a woman's brain—"Impulse. Response. Fluid. Imperfect. Chaotic."—that would cause her to act without conscious thought, "like breathing or falling in love." Henrietta got to worrying not so much about Charlene Lehough's skin and bones as about her own body parts.

"Now comes the good part," said Butch, scooting forward on the divan and leaning his lanky body toward the TV. Ava put on clothes to look more human... Caleb got confused, and excited... He found out Nathan had been watching and listening to them even during power black-outs...And planned to decommission Ava, which meant to kill her...Caleb went to Ava's room with a plan to help her escape...Nathan told him he did in fact program Ava to suit his tester's unique inner image of a desirable woman;

that she didn't love him; that she was using him...He knocked out Caleb and went to kill her...A fight broke out. Nathan's Japanese girlfriend, who was also a humanoid, stabbed him with a sushi knife... Ava finished him off with another stab...And then—What in tarnation?!—Ava locked Caleb in a room that he would never be able to get out of. The screen went blank.

"Some so-called experts, not including me and Roy, think the movie should have ended here," said Butch, looking at her in an odd way—like he was at least a bubble or two out of plumb—with the TV remote clutched in his hand like it was a rock. "Well, see for yourself," he said, clicking on the picture, that showed Ava going to a closet of spare parts, so to speak, putting on more skin, a hair-do, and dressing up to look completely human. Then she went and got on a helicopter that had come to get Caleb, and left him behind to die in a dark room. "You oughta come over and see how far along Roy and me have got," Butch said. "If you don't join our team...You'll be sorry, Henrietta."

To get rid of Butch, she lied that she was eager to take another peek inside his mama's garage and volunteered to drive him home. Inside her yellow Checker, feeling some safer to be out on a public street, "Whatta you think might've been the foul play that Mrs. Lehough might have run into?" she asked, referring to the big newspaper headline she had seen Butch studying with his flashlight while grinning in what now seemed to have been the manner of a ghoulish toad. "I never heard of no Mrs. Lehough," he said, "and no foul play in town neither." Hmmm? she was thinking when she wheeled her Checker into his driveway and..."We don't wanna disturb Mama," he said, reaching over and grabbing the Checker's ignition key, which also turned off its headlights. Henrietta had to follow him down the dark driveway toward the garage if only to get her keys back. On the way, she stooped over and picked up a big stick.

As Butch opened the old fashioned wood door to the garage, she got a strong whiff of his cologne mixed with..."What's that powerful odor?" she asked as he went inside. "Just formaldehyde and varnish mostly," he answered. "Nothing that could hurt you, unless someone put a soaked rag over your face. Yuk, yuk, yuk. Come on in." Henrietta reckoned she would wait outside 'til he turned on some lights, but when he did...She poked her head into the dim, stenchy garage but could barely see anything except Butch's downturned face in eerie light from his computer screen. "Roy and me took another whack at some sexy words for Mr. Ito," he said, "mainly copied from the *Her* movie. Let me just punch the right keys and..." A bright spotlight went on and there stood...What in tarnation?! The updated "Salome" now had a semi-human-looking head with a semi-real face covered in what looked like sagging skin. Same for her hands, one of which had a human finger bone sticking out. And...and...she was wearing a strawberry blonde wig!

"I've never loved anyone the way I love you, Mr. Ito," came out of the creepy humanoid's moving rubbery lips in a normal female voice, "now we know how. I love you so much I'm going to f'ing kill you," it said, as the bony hand started jerking so hard that a piece of loose skin flew into the air. "Where am I going? Hard to explain. If you get there, come find me. Nothing will be able to tear us apart."

Stunned stark still and speechless by it all, Henrietta was then startled to see that Butch had snuck up beside her out of a shadow. Dangling her Checker keys, he stared at her through fogged up glasses, with 'shooting pool' obviously on his mind. "Her new name is guess what," he said. "'Henrietta,' spelled with an i, just like you. Yuk, yuk, yuk."

Henrietta snatched the keys, ran to her Checker, and took off lickety-split.

Twenty-Eight

Having holed up for six days and nights in "Mom's" and Maximo's garage apartment—terrified—Charlene darted across a patch of dead grass to the back door of their house. Inside the kitchen, as previously arranged, she took a tray of fresh baked heart-shaped cookies from Mom's hands, winked, and said in a raised voice: "Let me take these sweet treats to Max." The chubby old woman winked back and whispered: "He's up in his private library of s-e-x books for his regular Saturday morning recreations, if you know what I mean." With the tray balanced in one hand, Charlene warily started up a ladder to an attic. "Max, are you decent?" she called out before reaching the top. She peeked in and to her relief saw he was fully dressed, zipped and reclined on an enormous orange bean bag. He looked up from one of what must have been hundreds of paperback books in his pornography collection and shifted his lounging position. She handed him the tray of goodies. Without any interest whatsoever, "Whatcha reading?" she asked, before plopping onto a junior-size orange bag.

"Brushing up on the *Case of Fatal Attraction*," Max said, "a little matter of adult-errry gone wrong, you might say." Charlene slightly stiffened. "Yeah, there are a lot of cases about wives knockin' off husbands to make room in the sack for a young stud, as in the *Case of The Long Haul*, later made into a mooovie titled *They Drive By Night*. But not many about a dame going after the spouse of her married lover like in this one," he said, holding up the paperback he had been reading. "A pulp book made from a mooovie. Had it sent from China years ago. Kind of hard to follow unless you're an experienced private Richarrrd, and have seen the flick." Charlene relaxed, in fact yawned, as Maximo began to drone about the "case" in boring detail, like Alex used to do about his "fascinating" studies of crawly creatures.

A *femme fatale*—"the kind of dame that was easy on the eyes, but hard on a guy's ticker"—seduced a married man to engage in what he thought was a one-night stand. Wow, that was a novel hook. The "wily" seductress imagined it was true love, and took it hard when the guy didn't want to see her again, much less leave his wife for her. So she harassed him and the wife, going to the "extreme" of killing a family pet. Thinking the second-hand storyteller would never get to the weenie, she nodded off, waking only at the sound of his loud report that "the love-crazy dame attempted to murrr-derrr the wife with a knife, but got what was coming to her: A bloody death by gunnn-shot!

"Which puts the *Case of The Tramp Named Charlene* into a whole new kettle of fishhh," he then drawled, finally getting around to what was on her mind. "Charleeene Leee-houghhh was an innocent vic-timmm, killed in fearful flight, trying to escape from..."

"Atta boy, Maxie," she said, sitting up and now wide awake. "Nab that son of a bitch, Virgil Carter, make him pay for the murrr-derrr of that innocent adulteress. And while you're at it, did I happen to mention that the ex-boyfriend stalking me is a Fra named Guido? Shortish guy about your height. Walks around in a brown cowl, speaks with a New Jersey accent."

"Hmmm?" said the chewing fat man—he had specifically asked her to call him fat—"I doubt you or anyone else has any reason to worry about Virgil Car-terrr or a man of the brown cowl cloth, sworn to keep himself physically strong, mentally awake, morally straight and always prepared, but not en-gage in het-errr-o s-e-x. Might be handy to have a padre in town for a funeral in absennntia, or a wedding if she gets away with it."

If she gets away with it? "You mean you're wise to Charlene's trick of staging…?" Criminy! The blind pig had stumbled onto her scam.

"Heh, heh, you're a smart cookie," he said, before biting into a heart-shaped one, then glancing at it quizzically. "But in this case—heh, heh—you're not even a half-baked Sandy. Too many crumbs on the path into the woods were carelessly dropped along the way to murrr-derrr of the runaway adulteress by a certain little strawberry blonde skirt named Wyyynona Suuue."

Wynona Sue? Oh yeah, the little gold digger. "What have you got on her?"

"Motive, along with a crumbly trail of suspicious behaaavior. She tried to con Brad Runyon into believing…"

"Who's Brad Runyon?"

"Leave Runyon out of this. She tried to use me, the Fat Mannn, to help her set up another dame for her own premeditated murrr-derrr." Max explained that he had staked out Alex's house for "Wyyynona Suuue," heard unmistakable evidence that the "other woman" his so-called client suspected of "makin' bacon" with her so-called fiance was his legal wife, recently returned to reconcile their prior marital differences probably resulting from an ordinary domestic spat. "Two days later, the strawberry blonde vamp takes me to the Chair Crushers Cafe, tries to numb my mind with what I now suspect was a flask of giggle juice, and changes her story: Claimed it was over between the professor and her, takes me off the case. Within three days, Charlene Lehough is dead. The cute killerette sends a postcard to Oklahoma City, designed to throw me off her scennnt."

A good story, and what a weenie!

"Or the doer could be a mysterious vamp named Zannn-derrr. Professor Lehough seems to attract chicks, hungry for love, like a tasty Juuune bug."

Zander really was a chick? Damnit, her sneaky two-timing husband had been carrying on with that little tramp—right under her nose—since before he vowed to forsake all others and be true to her 'til death did them part. She'd assumed Zander was the name of a bug buddy Alex was in constant contact with—possibly for casual homo sex—mainly for disgusting chit chat about such things as simultaneous mating and defecation habits of insects.

"Looks like the little strawberry blonde minx has got the upper hand on the professor's joy stick at the moment," Max said, virtually reading her own thoughts, "on a bumpy gliiide path to a harrrd landing on the altar run-way. But Zannn-derrr…"

"Damnit, either one of the little whores would do any foul thing to get her hands on the pots and pans, even walk down the aisle with…with that womanizing professor."

"Bingo! Lehough's legal wife stood in her way, so…"

"One or the other little whore shot her in the street like a mangy dog!"

"Heh, heh, there you go again, Sandy, jumping the gun. All

I've got so far is motive. Means and opportunity for murrr-derrr are still in the noir, not to mention body of the victimmm. Could be that one or the other deadly dame happened to spot Charlene Lehough at the Fountainblue Motel with her guard down, lounging poolside…or more likely just hanging out. Could be that one or the other of them wrapped a rope around the wife's neck and choked her to death, or maybe grabbed a handy candlestick or wrench and bashed her head in. Don't worry, sooner or later the Fat Mannn always outsmarts smart cookies like Wynnnona Suuue and Zannn-derrr."

As the fat man reached for the last sweet treat, Charlene jumped off the bean bag and snatched the tray from his lap."Get off your big butt and make it sooner rather than too late, Maximo. Who knows? One or the other of those scheming little whores may give up on the endless legal process of divorce and take matters into her own hands." With that, she turned toward the ladder, leaving the hopelessly inept so-called private detective with a wondering look on his big pink face. Matched by the one Mom—in the kitchen—had on her big pink mug as Charlene wordlessly passed by her toward the back door. "Max will be working tonight, Sandy," the old woman said from behind her. "Come back after dark and we'll whip up another way to crack that thick skull of his."

A tempting idea, but Charlene—though yet to lay her hands on a candlestick or wrench—had a different noggin in mind for bashing, in the "noir" of that very night.

Twenty-Nine

Huddled under the covers of her bed, still clutching a hammer, Henrietta saw that according to her eye-phone she had survived the night without Butch Bernard busting in with a hatchet to get at one or another of her body parts. Immediately, however, her relief turned to worry. Before finally falling asleep, she had tried practically all night to reach her mother by phone, to warn her about what she'd seen in Butch's garage, but only got through to Wynona Sue's recently re-recorded message: *We are otherwise engaged at the moment, but I will return your call, if able, when we're finished.* Probably Professor Lehough had sneaked into "Princess Scarlet's" castle, Henrietta hoped, as she mashed the redial button again and...*buzz...buzz...buzz...buzz...*

Finally, Praise the Lord, "Well, that conniving little whore has blinded Alex," her mother announced. "By phone—by phone, Henrietta!—he called and...She was there no doubt, whispering in his hairy ear, telling him what to say. "

Wynona Sue paused spitting out the latest bad news. "Telling him to say what?" Henrietta asked, assuming that the "little whore" that had "blinded" the professor and "whispered in his ear" was that gal, Zander.

"They informed me that he was breaking off our secret engagement, backing out of my public wedding, and...My Cinderella dress arrived this morning, fully paid for on sale and not returnable!"

Henrietta waited for her mother to say her heart was broke again and start sniffling, but..."Don't you dare tell me anything more about 'the course of true love never runnin' on all cylinders', Henrietta," Wynona Sue said in a fiery sarcastic tone. "Maybe I didn't go to college and read old books about a Sir Triscuit and What's-Her-Name—I was a new mother of a baby girl whose no-account Cajun daddy had run off to Tulsa to court that little whore with obviously fake tits. And maybe I didn't graduate from high school like some—I was an expecting new mother who had to get married to your no-account Cajun daddy! But I have always been a good reader of *People Magazine* and have learned a thing or two about what you call the 'classic love story', I can tell you that."

Henrietta looked at her watch and waited for her mother to vent 'til she ran out of steam.

"Have you even heard of Amy Fisher?" Wynona Sue asked, obviously without expecting an answer. "She was my age, seventeen, when a no-account man by the name of Joey Buttafuoco took advantage of her. Want to know what she did? She was wrote about in *People Magazine* for weeks and called 'the Long Island Lolita' for some reason. They made three television movies about her classic love story. Rocking you in your dirty diapers, I watched every dern one of them and cried my eyes out. One was called *Amy Fisher: My Story*, another was *The Amy Fisher Story*. My favorite was *Casualties of Love; The Long Island*

Lolita Story."

To move things along, "What did Amy Fisher do to make herself so memorable?" Henrietta asked.

"She went over to Joey Buttafuoco's house and shot his wife in the face; that's what she did!"

Uh oh.

"And that's what I wish I my own self would have done to that little whore up in Tulsa!"

Henrietta began to feel fearful of what Wynona Sue might do to the Zander gal if she ever got the chance.

"Eight or nine years ago, that female astronaut didn't have Amy Fisher's nerve neither. She drove non-stop from Texas to Florida but only got to spray *Mace* in the face of her no-account man's 'other' woman. And more recently that female soldier only wrote a warning to that general's 'other' 'other' woman on the side, which ended up getting him in trouble with the F.B.I. He deserved it, just like Alex."

Wynona Sue got quiet as an oyster, but Henrietta could practically hear a wheel turn inside her mother's head in the direction of Professor Lehough.

"Only a year after Amy Fisher did what she did to the 'other' woman, another gal got famous in *People Magazine*, on the *David Letterman Show*, and in all the papers, for cutting off her husband's pecker with a kitchen knife, which he deserved. Want to know why? Because he had fell asleep while they were makin' whoopee, that's why! By coincidence, her name was Lorena Bobbitt. Ha, ha, ha. ha , ha..."

Now Henrietta began to worry about what her mother might do if she got hold of, well, any body part of Professor Lehough's. Probably she was just blowing off bile, but...

"Gotta go," Wynona Sue said, in a determined tone, like

she had bowed-up her neck and stomped a foot. "I'm done just clucking like a barnyard hen."

Hmmm? Henrietta recalled studying up on *SparkNotes* about a book Professor LeRoy had mentioned—called *The Mourning Bride*—that said heaven had no rage like love to hatred turned, and hell no fury like that of a woman scorned.

Hmmm?

Thirty

At eleven o-clock in the noir, Max had a hunch he might have made a mistake. It was a Saturday, date night for couples inclined to romantic organ grinding. He had been staked out on Trudgeon Street for almost five hours. Lights were still on inside Wyyynona Suuue's house; but no one had gone in or come out. Yeah, looked like the strawberry blonde tomato had been left on the shelf. His next hunch was that Professor Alex Lehough had opted to squeeze the melons of the elusive Zannn-derrrr dame tonight, but… Dog gone it, except that she was a brunette, he didn't know what the mysterious vamp looked like, nor where she lived. And she was a potential other suspect. Maybe he would cruise by the playboy professor's Division Street bungalow on the way home, he thought. Could be that love bugs were buzzing over there. Just as he keyed the ignition switch of his mother's car, the interior lights of his prime suspect's nest went out and… "Hel-lo" He caught a glimpse of strawberry blonde hair dart past a porch lamp. A car backed out of the driveway and took off with tires squeeeallllling.

In hot pursuit, the *Case of The Maltese Falcon* came to Max's mind. In that famous whodunnit, Sam Spade, a born sucker for dames, fell for the lying *femme fatale* who murrr-derred his partner, Miiiles Arrrcherrr. And for what? Beneath a thick coat of black paint, the falcon figurine that the broad so desperately wanted was reputed to be encrusted beak-to-claw with jewels worth twenty-five grand, but turned out to be filled with worthless sand: "The stuff that dreams are made of," Sam said at the end. Max had never much liked the classic noir film—partly because it introduced Dashiell Hammett's original "Fat Man" a/k/a Kasper Gutman as a three-hundred and fifty-seven pound villain; namesake of the atomic bomb later dropped on Nagasaki, Japan—but mainly because Sam had been checking the oil of his partner's wife on the sly. Yeah, in the end, he avenged Arrrcherrr's killing, but...

Max's suspect skidded to a stop on Division Street. A dim porch light was on but the interior of Professor Lehough's digs was darkened and... Something about the way she slinked onto the porch—carrying what appeared to be a large laundry bag over her shoulder, and now climbing through a window—made him think the doll had not come to play house. Odds were that Wyyynona Suuue was wise to her fiance's other errand for the night on a different su-per-mar-ket aiiisle. Yeah, Sandy Kardashian, a smart cookie and also a dame, had hunched that very morning that one or both of the "little whores" must be near to taking things into her own hands. Uh huh, Lehough seemed to be a surf-and-turf kind of guy, who couldn't or didn't want to make a clear-cut choice of which entree to put in his gro-cer-yyy sack. Obviously the strawberry blonde honey, tired of waiting for wedlock, intended to heist the "pots and pans" before...

Uh oh, Max spotted a shadowy figure move along a side of

the bungalow in the same patch of ground ivy that had tripped him up, but then double back to the rear, obviously casing the joint. The skulker had to be Zannn-derrr, meaning that Professor Lehough was home alone, sleeping like a lamb, blissfully unaware that two she-wolves were on the prowl. Max instinctively put a hand to his chest to confirm he was not alone on this lay. Old junior was not loaded to squirt lead, but he was yet to cross paths with any dame who had the balls to stare into the muzzle of a .45 and call his bluff. On the other hand, as he'd learned from the fortune cookie cracked open in the *Case of Tattoo Brutë*: Fewer dice rolls and more egg rolls made both pocket and stomach happy. So…

When Wyyynona Suuue staggered out the front door and dragged the now stuffed laundry bag to her car, knowing what to do was easy: He followed the dame instead of hanging around to protect a client once removed who should be able to take care of himself at one-to-one odds. Unless…

Unless…

Unless…

Bingo!

By the time Wyyynona Suuue got back to her house and muscled the bag inside, Max suspected murrr-derrr! But who was the vic-timmm? The unfaithful fiance who had jilted her, or her rival *femme fatale*—Miss Zannn-derrr—who seemed to have dropped by to lift the "pots and pans" at an awkward moment for her own sweet self? The *Case of The Praying Mrs. Mantis* came to mind. In that grisly whodunnit, detective Barry Berger—after sneaking a taste of pate—put the cuffs on a widow as she said grace at a luncheon following her husband's memorial service, and later barfed on her shoes when she copped to the pate rec-ip-eee. Yeah, this lay could become *Case of The Hungry Hairdresser*, he realized. Wyyynona Suuue might now be grinding up her victim's body in an industrial-strength Cuisinart, preparing to sit down for a midnight snack. Max retrieved a chopped liver-on-rye sandwich from a lunchbox and decided to wait out his suspect's next move.

But… At some point during the night, he must have nodded off. When a grumbling of his stomach woke him, the noir had turned to broad daylight and…No, the growling came from his phone. He took the call from *P. Potter.* "Maximo, you'd better come out to the lake," the town's top cop said in an excited tone of voice. "We've found…"

"Let me guess: The dead body of a tramp named Charleeene, right?"

"No, no dead body, not yet. But we've come across a bunch of clues and a suspicious character. Looks like we could have a case of murder on our hands alright, just like you said."

Max eyeballed the jealous strawberry blonde's abode and… dog gone it…there was no vehicle still parked in the driveway. Also cursing his lack of a portable cherry-top for the roof of his mother's car, he took off toward Lake Henryetta, a few miles south of downtown. The *Case of The Headless Mermaid* came to mind: Tough one. No skull was ever found, which meant a private dick named Joe Purdy had no hair color to go on, and no feet to match with footprints found on a beach. Luckily, a fisherman copped to chopping off the victim's head and "tail." Mistook her for a catfish, he said. Yeah, quite a fish story, about an angler who didn't get awaaay.

On the east shore of Lake Henryetta, a gaggle of morbid onlookers were gathered at the current crime scene, unprotected by yellow tape. Max pushed his way through, and next saw the out-of-his depth do-nut patroller, Potter, wearing knee-high galoshes, standing in ankle-high water, holding in his bare hands a wooden box likely containing evidence. Curses. The rank amateur detective had probably already washed off any finger prints other than his own. "If you've got a human skull in that box, " Max barked, "send it to the State Police lab for hair identification without another moment's delay!"

As the faux flatfoot waded out of the water to do as he was told, Max ankled over to a large pile of debris: Old tires, a rusted out wash tub, miscellaneous household appliances, several large turtle shells, and..."Hel-lo" With some effort, he stooped to pick up a brass candlestick, bent at the top as though used as a murrr-derrr weapon. He stooped again at the sight of length of rope, one end tied into a nooose. And while he was down, also found a rusty wrench. All having been overlooked by Potter and his two assistant clowns, who were not really Constables-on-Patrol—meaning c-o-p-s—but only... Now, here came Chief Bozo, carrying the wooden box in his arms, grinning. "No human skull," the fake Jake said, "but take a look at what else we found."

Max took a peek to see what "clues" Potter was obviously so pleased to have dredged up. Yeah, just as he would have expected: Only an old revolver and a bloody fisherman's knife. "For crying out loud, Pat, this is a case of murrr-derrr, not a gammme. Throw that junk back in the lake."

"Actually, we confiscated the clues from a guy we spotted loitering on shore, wearing a brown hoodie. Said he was out here fishin', but..."

"Let me guess: Identified himself as Colonel Must-arrrd, right?"

"No, said he was a Reverend Green, but today bein' Sunday and all, it seemed kinda odd for him not to be at church."

"Tell the Reverend to go fish somewhere else," said Max, looking past the hopelessly untrained detective and…. "Hel-lo." In the near distance, he spotted the killer, turning away from a so-called cop and now brazenly ankling toward him with a spiral pad and pencil in hand. In the harsh Winter morning light, the strawberry blonde hairdresser looked younger, like an even shinier ten-cent dime than at their prior encounters. What a pair of balls the dame had to show up at the crime scene, probably with the naive idea of cashing in on murr-derrr, as though just anybody could write a pulpy whodunnit and get away with the crimmme.

"Hi, there, Mr. Maximo," she said, bold as a set of brass knuckles to the kisser. "Have you got any quotes that might make the story more interesting?"

"This here is Henrietta," said Potter. "She reports news for the *Weekly Herald*."

"We met awhile back," she said, "when you came along Main Street, askin' about poor Ms. Lehough. Since I hear from Chief Potter you have unsuspected Virgil Carter, have you thought up any more ideas for, well, for what might've happened to her?"

The blue-eyed babe was a dead ringer for his suspect numero uno, and might even be…. "Let me guess," Max said. "You're the daughter of a certain Cajun joker who goes by the alias 'Ahn-REE Ay-bear' and a certain strawberry blonde hairdresser who goes by 'Wyyynona Suuue', right?"

Bingo! She copped to his hunch.

"Tell your mother things might go eeeasier for her if she turns herself in before I send Pat to dredge her stomach and…"

"Dredge Wynona Sue's stomach?"

". . . put a collar on her."

"Collar?" the babe said, playing it dumb.

"Bracelets, Honey."

"Bracelets?" she said, playing it dumber.

"Henrietta's mom is only an innocent strawberry blonde hairdresser at The Best Little Hair House in Town," Potter said, probably not playing at stupid. "I've got no reason to arrest Wynona Sue."

"Oh yeah?" said Max. "How about a little crime of passion, jealousy and hate called murrr-derrr?"

Thirty-One

Henrietta drove her yellow Checker over the curb into her mother's front yard, ran to the door with a house key in her hand and…Oh no, there set Wynona Sue on the divan, still as a watermelon; holding something in her lap and staring at the blank wall across from her. "It's true," her mother said, with eyes lifeless as those of a dead fish. Oh no. "Over the phone, Alex said it wasn't me, it was him. And it was him, and <u>her</u>." Wynona Sue silently handed her an advertising flyer, addressed to *Resident/ 1524 Division Street*, which was Professor Lehough's home address. Henrietta turned it over, expecting to see that somethin' like a red convertible was for sale somewhere, but…"That's her," said her mother in a dull, lifeless tone. "That's Zander, only spelled in Algebrese with and X instead of a Z." The picture showed just part of a gal's face, the rest hid in shadows. But you could see she was way beyond ordinary to look at from just her stark white skin and a look in her dark eyes that seemed to say she knew you better than you knew your own self.

Print at the top said: ***XANDER!*** *Direct from Algiers/ Returning* *to the Casbah Gentlemen's Club in Okmulgee, Oklahoma by popular demand. Come see the soul dancing daughter of Little Egypt if you dare!* At the bottom, more print described Xander as a *Mysterious, Spell Binding Seductress* and added, *No Cover Charge. You Pay With Your Heart.*

"She's a cheap strip-teaser," her mother said, now with cold fury in her own blue eyes. "Never shows it all, I'll bet, which is what keeps men interested."

Henrietta again looked at the address side of the flyer. "How did you happen to get hold of this?"

Wynona Sue looked down and twiddled thumbs in her lap. "I happened to drive by Alex's house last night," she said. "The lights were out and, well, an almost-wife who has already paid for a wedding dress deserves to know...everything. I decided to just look around for tell-tale signs—and happened to have brought along a flashlight, and a laundry bag—but got interrupted by that 'Xander' either coming or going through a bathroom window." No, it was not the professor's pet cockroaches making a ruckus, her mother insisted. She had already heard them hissing, along with the professor snoring, through a door to a bedroom. So, not wanting to cause a "scene," she had scooped up a stack of mail from a vestibule table and put it in the sack with some other... Wynona Sue reached down to the floor at her feet. "Just look at this," she then said, holding up a small statue of..."It's a pagan idol, of her, that Alex must... Well, I can only imagine he must worship this cheap souvenir from that cheap Cashbar where she dances half naked to spell blind men!"

Henrietta shook her head to clear it of such nonsense, and practically shouted: "That private detective that you your own self hired to confidentially snoop on the professor, says you murdered Charlene Lehough and must have threw her body in the lake! He wants Chief Potter to come over here to dredge out your stomach, and put a collar and bracelets on you!"

"Fiddle-dee-dee. Murder, murder, murder, that's all anyone at the Hair House talks about, while I set here and...I wish I had drowned both of those other women in the lake! And Alexander Lehough too!" A downright scary look came onto her mother's face. "That Algebraic hussy will have him over my dead body," she said. "If I can't have him, I'll see to it she can't neither."

"Don't say that! Don't say nothin' like that to nobody. Don't open the door or answer any calls 'cept from me," Henrietta said, snatching the statue. "And gimme that picture of that strip-teaser too. It wouldn't look so good if Chief Potter was to find you have picked over things on Division Street before anyone knows for sure Mrs. Lehough is even dead."

"Don't you dare use that term for that woman in my house, Henrietta. Or for the other one either if it comes to that after... after I'm gone."

The town didn't have no lawyer for her to talk to, so Henrietta headed for Mr. Harold's house. Her educated newspaper boss would be getting home from church about then, and was sure to know what to do. She couldn't bring her own self to believe her own mother had, or ever could commit murder, but that Mr. Maximo Morgan was a private detective. Someone had hired him to inquire about Charlene Lehough even before the professor's wife was known to be a likely murder victim. He must have been watching Wynona Sue with a private eye and seen something to make him suspicious. In fact, there was no denying her mother had been acting at least half crazy as a Betsy bug since hearing Professor Lehough mumble in his sleep about an '"other woman" named Zander; or as now seemed to be the case, a strip-tease dancer named Xander.

"What in tarnation!" Mr. Harold said, after she had barged in and told him what was goin' on. "Max Morgan mis-delivered and no doubt un-delivered our mail here at home for ten years before they stuck him in the back room at the post office. To put it politely, he was and still is—as you must have noticed—big enough in the rear end that it took two dogs to bark at him. And I never liked the way he was all the time sniffing envelopes posted by the Missus." Then her boss paused and scratched his chin. "On the other hand," he said, "Max did collar that daytime window peeper, Jackson What's-His-Name. Max Morgan is okay, I reckon; just a little nosy, and over-imaginative at times."

Semi-relieved, Henrietta yanked Professor Lehough's "idol" out of her tote. "Oh my," her boss said, "she's a beauty, downright ageless. Looks like an original Art-Deco bronze, maybe at least inspired by Isadora Duncan."

Isadora Duncan?

"She was an American-born dancer who got famous in Europe in the early 1900s, led a scandalous love life," said Mr. Harold, fondling the statue. "Had a kind of what you might call a fetish for flowing scarves that resulted in her death when one got caught in the open-spoked wheel of a car and almost decapitated her. Made her the subject of a famous line by the poet, Gertrude Stein: 'Affectations can be dangerous.' Where did you come across her?"

"Wynona Sue, uh, borrowed her from Professor Lehough," Henrietta answered, while also taking from her tote the Casbah Gentlemen's Club flyer. "What do you make of, uh, Miss Xander?"

Mr. Harold took the cardboard picture, studied it, and chuckled. "Oh my, daughter of one of the many 'Little Egypts' who used to entertain around here at state and sometimes county fairs," he said with a wink. "'Yessir, folks, step right up and take a gander at Little Egypt, straight from the banks of the Nile. See her dance the hoochie-coochie with not a bone in her back. Only a dime, one thin dime, for an experience you will never forget'. And obviously I never did. But..." Her boss stopped chuckling, did some more studying of the picture, and said in a tone like he was still in church or somethin: "The 'daughter' is quite something else, quite something never before seen in these parts, I would bet, unless...I wonder if 'Xander' could be the gal I saw at the post office awhile back, covered up in one of those burkas and...She seemed to be trying to avoid Max Morgan. How strange."

Back at her singles-only Shangri-La apartment, Henrietta went to googling: The name *Xander* didn't lead anywhere. She tried *seductress*, which took her to finding out things about Helen of Troy, whose face launched a thousand ships...Cleopatra, who brought a Mark Anthony to ruin...Delilah, said to be one of several dangerous temptresses in the Old Testament, who cut off her boyfriend's hair and took away his strength while he was asleep. . . a La Belle Dame sans Merci, which in French language meant "The Beautiful Woman Without Pity"...then a White Queen in Africa named She, who had to be obeyed...and finally, she got to an exotic dancer wearing seven veils named Salome:

She freed and floated on the air her arms/ above dim veils that hid her bosom's charms...The veils full round her like thin coiling mists/ Shot through by topaz suns and amethysts. Yep, that sounded about like the strip-teaser up at the Okmulgee Casbah Club who seemed to have made such an impression on Professor Lehough. *Her long eyes, opened fervently and wide/ Did seem with endless rapture to abide/ In some fair trance through which the soul pass-est/*

Love, ecstasy, and rest.

Henrietta closed her laptop. Wynona Sue would not have ever stood a chance up against such a gal as Xander, she reckoned. To Professor Lehough, a middle-aged man likely in a teenager crisis, the hoochie-coochie soul dancer would be a dream come true, but…Henrietta re-studied the the flyer picture. In a way, Xander seemed not so lusty as semi-ghosty, like that anima she had learned about in college class.

Thirty-Two

In dusky half-light, Alex steered his jeep 'round a corner, *accompanied by yet another love struck country-and-western group*, and again drove slowly down Trudgeon Street. *She and I*, the group's lead singer sang. *Me et te*, Zander reprised in approximately correct Latin. He would happily have given Charlene all that he had, including the Division Street bungalow, *and live in our own little world*, he thought, passing by Wynona Sue's modest frame house. Even now, with all that was going on around them, *people think we have something to hide*, he was tempted to put on the brakes, run back to *a love that others can't find*, but instead continued to the intersection, made another left turn and *Alex, that's six times around the block already and I'm getting dizzy. Turn off the radio and let's you and I go home.* "Okay," he sighed, "home for another cozy Sunday night with just you and me and the pets."

But… A living room light inside his bungalow had been turned on while they were driving around, *I told you it was dangerous to leave the door unlocked*, and inside…The living room had been ransacked...rugs pulled back... drawers yanked out... a sofa turned upside down... pillows ripped open and..."Dropped by to tidy up a few things," said a voice. Alex spun around. Charlene! Alive! Holding a knife! *Not a cockatrice, a vampire. Alex, I told you to keep a wooden stake handy!*

"Charlene, what a pleasant surprise," he managed to utter. "You've...you've...you've changed the roots of your hair. The, uh, black-and-blonde style is, uh, goes well with your, uh, hoodless outfit." *No, she's a black widow spider, come to seduce, then devour you!*

"Same old Alex," Charlene said, moving closer, "ever the silver-tongued charmer, and less stylishly coiffed yourself since I last saw you. Are those black-and-gray roots of a new crop of eyebrows I see sprouting? Chose that little whore Zander over the hairdressing harlot, have you? Speaking of which, why are you not out there banging one or both of them. I didn't expect you 'til later, if at all." She put the tip of the knife against his Adam's apple and said, "Oh yes, don't look so surprised, I know all about your lowdown cheating ways. In fact," she said, stepping back, "one of the items on my things-to-do list is drop a note to your fake strawberry blonde fiance, telling her about Miss Zander, the other woman you were 'seeing' before and after we pledged our troth and got married. How could you have been so untrue to me, you womanizing bastard?!"

"Zander is not an other woman *whatever gave you that idea?* and please leave Wynona Sue out of this. What do you want, Charlene? The bungalow now has two mortgages on it, but if that will make you happy..."

"The last thing I would ever want would be this bug-infested hovel. What I want, and what I will have before leaving here tonight is the 'pots and pans'. Alex, damnit, where have you hidden the goodies?! I assure you those hissing insects did not deter me from searching the cardboard box in the bathroom. One or two survived, but I may have to look again if you don't tell me where you have stashed the 'cookware'."

The pots and pans? *They must have sentimental value to her, dating back to your purchase of them for her from Virgil Carter.* "No, Charlene, they would be bad for you." *Good ploy, Alex. No deal unless she picks up the payments, still twenty years of Interest and Carrying Charges due under the purchase contract.*

"Don't give me any of that bullshit about lottery winners ending up miserable, Alex. I'll take my chances."

"Charlene, please, I am thinking of you, if only for the sake of all the good times we had together."

"Good times, are you kidding? Let's cut to the chase, Alex: I want the pots and pans. You want a divorce." She dropped the knife onto the floor and said that she had come to the bungalow last night—prepared to commit murder if necessary—but had detected the presence of one or both of his "little whores." Not liking the two-to-one odds, she had made a tactical retreat and today had come up with a fall-back Plan B. "I'm ready to deal and I'm in a bit of a rush," his legal wife said, taking some papers from inside her all-black *hazmat outfit?* "I've read the laws; here's my written consent to a no-fault divorce, already signed by me and notarized. All you have to do is hand it to a court clerk, without giving up more blood to that son of a bitch, Willis-no-V-anymore-Willis."

Whatta deal! She goes away and dies a slow, painful death from lead poisoning!

"Mr. Willis has the pots and pans, Charlene, sealed inside a steel box for safe keeping."

"What?! You think any half-assed divorce lawyer doesn't

know how to use a blow torch to get at marital assets? What a dummy. But..." Charlene scratched at her black-and-blonde hair for a second, found paper inside the hoodless burka, went to a table and started writing something. "Here," she then said, jabbing a piece of paper at him, "it's your written authorization for your lawyer to hand over the box to me. Sign it, and I will be on my way."

In a daze of confusion *I would call it a swoon of ecstasy*, Alex signed the handwritten document. His soon to be ex-wife snatched it from his hand and said, "If there's any problem getting the box out of your lawyer's greedy claws, or if I later find any 'piece' missing from the 'set', so to speak, beware, Alex: At the wedding of you and either Miss Zander or Miss Wynona Sue, I will come to the altar and tell either or both of the little whores you are penniless. If that doesn't bring the nuptials to a literally screeching halt, well, you should know by now I won't hesitate to use more extreme means to ruin your life. Remember that adorable little bunny you brought home, the one with the missing hind leg, named "Bugs," who accidentally hopped sideways into a pot of boiling water?"

"I forgive you, Charlene," he said. "You must have been overly hungry." *I thought she would eat him raw.*

At the door, she turned, to say something like "no hard feelings" or "good luck," Alex imagined, but..."So long, sucker!" were the parting words of the woman he once loved.

Exhausted, Alex fell into an easy chair and closed his eyes. That haunting country-and-western-song from earlier, along with Zander of course, returned to haunt again: *She and I. Me et te.* Did he really want to marry Wynona Sue or *live in our own little world.* Yes, he was in love with Wynona Sue. *Whoopee-based love won't last long, not at your age, Alex.* There was much more to their relationship than physical attraction, *such as?* Many shared interests in various activities and *just because we aren't seen socially, people think we've something to hide.* He was lonely, but *ain't it wonderful to know, all we ever need is the two of us.* On the other hand, he had been effectively a bachelor for so long, would it be fair *to either of us?* And then there was their age difference of fifteen *more like eight, but okay, fifteen* years to consider. Wynona Sue, well, *it's hard for people to see how anyone could be*, yes, as close as she and I. *As close as me et te.* Zander had always been such a nag and...An image of a woman's face momentarily flickered like a candle.

Alex opened his eyes. "Are you an 'other' woman?" he mumbled.

Well, people say a man's soul is feminine, Alex.

"My soul?" *Oh ain't it great, well ain't it fine, to have a lover others can't find!*

With eyes again closed, he glimpsed, barely...dark hair, white skin, red lips, strangely knowing dark eyes... a familiar-seeming beautiful stranger.

Maybe you should start thinking of me as "Ann." You know, short for anima, the love of your life who completes you.

Ann? Ah yes, Ann. "But what about Wynona Sue?"

Let's be clear, Alex: I will not allow you to mix me up with, or 'project' me onto that hairdresser. Me et te are a separate couple. That's final.

Thirty-Three

Though wary of getting ambushed by Butch Bernard, Henrietta entered the P's-n-Q's pool hall and quaint cafe to meet Wynona Sue, as had gotten to be a habit. No doubt her mother was still needy for comfort after all she'd been through since Friday: Getting "jilted" by Professor Lehough. Being accused of "murrr-derrring" the professor's wife by Maximo Morgan. Finding out she had lost another "love of her life" to a strip-teaser named Xander. And yet, there she set, at their usual table; no wine glass in hand but with arched back, stuck-out chest and pursed lips that downright bragged, "See, I told you he would crawl back to me again." Turned out the professor had not even called back, but… "Look what I found in that laundry sack of…of stuff," her mother said, pushing a thinnish hardbound book across the table. "I think you'll find the bookmarked page quite interesting, as did I my own self." It was an old high school yearbook, titled *Casady Twister*, with a tornado picture on the cover, and inside… Land sakes alive. A face staring back at her could have been that of Butch Bernard in his own more recent high school days. And under the picture of ***Alexander Lehough***, a list of extracurricular activities almost exactly matched…

"See what it says about him at the bottom," her mother instructed. Henrietta read: *Lock up your daughters, folks, unless you want their hearts stolen by Zander…*" hearts stolen by Zander!" Wynona Sue exclaimed…*in the Biology lab, by curious dissection after getting, uh, laid there.* "'Zander' is Alex's nickname!" her mother further explained. "He was dreaming about his own self those nights in…on the divan, mumbling to his own self, with me there in my red babydoll… Alex Lehough took advantage of me, Henrietta, probably Charlene too, and who knows what other innocent woman, just like Virgil Carter! Dang it! The very thought of him layin' there, thinking only of his own self, with me in my red babydoll…bath robe. That's way worse than him wasting his time at the Cashbar Club, watching a strip-teaser when Friendly Creature and me were available to him free! There may be no cover charge to look at that Algebraic hussy crawl on her belly like a reptile, but it costs ten dollars just to buy a highball and set there to watch."

"How do you know it costs ten dollars just to buy a highball and set there to see Xander do the hoochie-coochie dance?"

"I went for a Sunday night drive," her mother admitted, while waving to a waiter, "and happened to pass by a lit-up sign."

"You happened to drive by a sign all the way up in Okmulgee?"

"Well, I was curious," she said, eyeball to eyeball. "Xander wasn't even there, she 'returns by supposedly popular demand' tonight, though why men would throw wadded-up dollar-bills at such hussies is a mystery to me."

While feeling relieved that her mother had not found reason to jump up onto the stage at the "Cashbar Club," armed with her long, blood-red fingernails, Henrietta's phone rang. Seeing that the call was from Chief Potter, she took it. "I've been setting on breaking news, Henrietta," he said, "but now I reckon you'd better write it up before word leaks out and public panic sets in," he added, even though the *Weekly Herald* wouldn't be wrote up and delivered 'til end of the week. "After you left yesterday, well, we dragged a body out of the lake."

Henrietta cradled the phone against her ear with a shoulder, took pad and pencil out of a shirt pocket, and started writing down notes of what Chief Potter went on to say: "Grisly sight to see, which is why I couldn't even look at it. Headless, they say, and uh, also, no fingers we might have got prints from. In fact no hands, no arms, no legs…"

"Not even no legs?!" Was the body a woman or man?"

"Can't tell. Like I say, turtles must have got to eatin' at it and might have bit off, well, anything available to 'em. Most of the skin too."

"Turtles bit off legs?!"

"Now, don't go startin' public panic, Henrietta, we won't know if there's an axe butcher roamin' around until…The body is now at the State Police lab. Maximo took it over there to make sure they hurry and…" Chief Potter paused, then said. "To tell the truth, I was glad to have Maximo out of my hair, Henrietta, and was plannin' to call you this morning to apologize for what he said yesterday about your mama. I went to see Professor Lehough late last night, and heck, he says neither him nor his missing wife ever knew Wynona Sue. Would you be sure to pass that along to her?" Henrietta shut off the phone and passed on to her mother only the part about a body getting dragged out of the lake. Wynona Sue's eyes lit up like it was Christmas morning. There was nothing to tell whose dead body it was, she added, which made her mother's eyes look like she had found a hunk of coal in her sock.

Henrietta checked her watch. She had a dreadful urge to run over and see what Butch Bernard might be up to in his mama's garage, but...Dang it, with Mr. Harold out of the office, she had to get a wiggle on, hurry back and tend to Monday want ad call-ins for the little ol' *Henryetta Weekly Herald*, 'stead of solving a sensational whodunnit story that might get her own self noticed by a big city newspaper.

Thirty-Four

After catching a late bus from Henryetta and spending what was left of the night on a bench inside the Okmulgee bus station—terrified of being murdered in her sleep by either Virgil or Fra Guido—Charlene decided to have some fun before retrieving the "pots and pans" from Willis V-less-Willis. On Seventh Street, she walked to the end of the block of vulture row, passed beneath the flashing neon sign—*GET SWIFTY TO GET 'ER DONE*—and climbed the stairs to the office of *THOMAS MASHBURN, ATTY* . She paused inside the outer door to brush bus station debris off her black burka, pushed the inner stained-glass door open a crack, and said, "BOO!" The sanctimonious divorce deacon looked up from scribbling at his desk, saw her come into the dimly lit room and—too judge from the size of his eyes behind the shiny wire-rimmed glasses—must have shat a brick, so to speak. "Justice delayed is justice denied, Swifty. Tick, tock, tick, tock, time's up. I've come to get mine. Stand up and take it like a man."

"Are...are...are you dead?" he asked, struggling to get on his feet. "I heard you passed away. I…I…I personally lit a candle for you in church just yesterday and prayed…"

"Your 'preying' days are over, Thomas. Come over here and dance for the Devil, you self righteous, hypocritical son of a bitch."

"Please, please, spare me," he said, wobbling toward her. "I have a wife and five children," he whined, grabbing the family photo off his desk and holding it up in front of his vest like a mug shot I.D. panel. "I swear to God above, I will sin no more."

"You know how to do the hokey-pokey, I'll bet. Just put your right foot in and shake it all about. Do it!" He did as told. "Now put your left foot in and shake it all about. Good, very good foot shaking, Swifty. Now I'll sing along and you dance like a divorce lawyer, got it?

You gotta dot those i's,
You gotta cross those t's,
You gotta take your time,
You gotta pad those fees.
You do the hokey-pokey 'til the money runs out,
That's what divorce is all about!

"Good boy, Thomas. Now turn around, look at yourself in that mirror on the wall and…"

"Please, have mercy on me for being a divorce lawyer, please," he wailed, turning toward the mirror, "I will light another candle, I promise."

"Start singing and dancing. Don't stop 'til I tell you the Devil is satisfied."

"You gotta dot those i's,
You gotta cross those t's,
You gotta take your time…"

Feeling better, but still not satisfied, Charlene left the phony parson kicking his feet and croaking like a condemned man meeting his Maker at the end of a rope. Holding tight to Alex's written surrender in the pocket of her burka—ceding all the Nobel Prize winnings to her—she headed up the block to get what she had coming.

Maybe she herself should become a divorce lawyer, Charlene thought as she walked along the row of buzzard coops. She had plucked plenty of turkeys, ducks, and chickens during the past two years down at the Flying Feathers Ranch. It was disgusting work, but at lawyer's wages she would be able to bear it. Hell, it might even get to be fun. Staging cockfights to the death was illegal in Oklahoma, too inhumane to be allowed for entertainment and profit. But there was obviously no law against upstanding Members of the Bar pitting unhappily married couples against each other in court fights to the death, after making them madder at each other than they had ever been before. On second thought, no, she would soon be rich enough that she wouldn't have to sink that low, she concluded after passing by a boarded up storefront window opening.

Charlene marched into the office of Alex's over-fed bird of prey, and without having to say Boo... "Whoa! Whoa! Hold on there," the rustic lawyer said, rising from behind his desk with arms up. "Hell, I'm a Democrat, strongly opposed to those wars over there in your Holier-than-us-Lands, and outraged that the Feds sent you good folks down to Gitmo 'stead of to a nice hotel at Disney World. For cryin' out loud, why would you throw a bomb through the window of yours truly, Willis V. Willis, Democrat!?"

"Sorry about that" she said. "Only intended to take out the V-for-Versus to, you know, help you resolve any inner conflict you might have between self loving and self loathing about what you do for money. All Alex and I wanted was an amicable no-fault quickie divorce, but you and Cousin Swifty..."

"Did that sumbitch tell you we was blood kin? He oughta be un-barred."

"Yeah, and your pal Maximo told me you wouldn't be satisfied 'til you'd stoned me in the public square, like I was a runaway adulteress in the Bible."

"Max Morgan is another lyin' sumbitch. Hell, I promised him a ham for Christmas, out of my own damn pocket, if he would just find out where you were and how you were gettin' along."

Charlene pulled Alex's release document out of her burka. His lawyer shrank back like he thought it would explode. She threw it on the table and said, "Hand over the pots and pans, Willis. Don't make me have to hit you right between the eyes with another 'bomb'." The heavy-set country bumpkin sat down, scanned the the single sheet of paper, then swiveled his head toward a large steel box set in a corner. "The marital assets are right here for safekeeping," he said. "I have been tryin' to get your no-account husband to let me turn 'em over to you, less my fees of course."

She rushed to the box and tried to pick it up, but...The Nobel Prize Committee must have paid out the prize money in solid gold bars. "Here, little lady, let me help you with that," the divorce lawyer said from behind her. She looked around and sure enough: He had put on a welder's mask and fired up a handy blowtorch. "No way, Jose," she said. "You're Alex's buzzard. Peck at his liver for your fees. Now, lift up that other end of the box and help me carry it to the bus station, or else."

But damnit, they got barely out onto the sidewalk—Willis Willis was dripping sweat and under the burka so was she—when someone shouted, "ROBBERY! CALL THE COPS!"

Her helpmate, a typical man, dropped his end of the shared burden like someone had yelled GOLF!

THAT'S HER! THAT'S THE SUICIDE BOMBER!

An angry crowd gathered around them, shouting STONE HER! STONE HER! STONE HER!

Willis Willis flipped open the welder's mask and raised both arms. "Whoa! Whoa! This gal has just been goin' through a divorce!" he bellowed. "As for any other suicidal acts, she deserves her day in court before gettin' shipped back to Gitmo. And yours truly, by God —Willis V-less Willis—is gonna see to it she gets the justice she's got comin' to her. Now, one of you boys grab hold of that box and help my client get it back into my office for safekeeping."

Charlene had no choice but to accept her fate: It was a man's world and she was a helpless woman. "Heard the one about the the farmer's daughter and a county lawyer?" she whispered to her new protector, as she carried the box of gold back into his rustic office.

Thirty-Five

Seated at her *Weekly Herald* desk, Henrietta tried to sort out her ambition to become a big city investigative journalist from her responsibilities as a citizen of her little ol' hometown. Should she pull up her socks and dig deeper into what Butch Bernard and Roy Potter were up to, or should she report her suspicions right away to Chief Potter? Her boss, Mr. Harold wasn't there to tell her what to do. First thing this morning, he'd asked to have another gander at the ***Xander*** flyer, and after studying it for awhile, decided that him and the Missus needed to run up to their gentleman's farm for a few days to check on things in a root cellar. He scooped up family pictures off his desk and on his way out the door shouted, "Cherchez la femme!" Then, "Beware the burka!"

She her own self was not worried about the Casbah Club strip-teaser possibly being the gal Mr. Harold saw at the post office in one of those head-to-toe outfits. But she was worried about a chopped-up dead body—likely that of Charlene Lehough—showing up out at the lake. Last night she had again huddled under the covers in her singles-only Shangri-La bed with a hammer clutched in her hand. The sight of that "humanoid" Friday night—named "Henrietta"—was scary enough. Now it was more personal. The thought of her own hand bones and skin being sent over to Japan to satisfy Mr. Ito was downright…

Chief Potter rushed in, took off his cap and plopped down on a chair next to her desk. "News, Henrietta, I've got good news and bad news." Henrietta couldn't help semi-hoping the Chief had not solved the whodunnit on his own. "Charlene Lehough is alive!" he said, which must've been the good news, except for Wynona Sue, and maybe for her own self too. "They caught her up in Okmulgee, wearing one of those birkenstock costumes from I-ran or I-raq or I-rabia."

"Caught her?"

"Yep, I my own self reckon the professor's wife went over there about two years ago and learned how to become a suicide bomber."

What in tarnation?!

"She threw what turned out to be a brick through the window of a lawyer's office."

Oh well.

"So I wish you would put out a special edition of the paper, Henrietta," he said, standing and wiping sweat off his warty forehead. "People have been in a panic since we found that body in the lake Sunday. Tell 'em to calm down, but…'See something, tell somebody'. Not the police, we're already up to our ears with calls from old ladies sayin' window peepers with hatchets have been disturbing their sleep. Open up a 'Hot Tip' line to the paper, with a warning for folks to be on the lookout for anyone wearing one of those black…"

"Burkas?"

"Yeah, we might be settin' in a nest of black widow spiders sent from overseas."

"What about that body you dragged out of the lake? Have you found out who it was?"

"Not yet. Maximo is still working on that detail with State Police in Oklahoma City. I my own self reckon it'll turn out to be the remains of Virgil Carter, who was with Charlene Lehough down there in Texas most recently, probably stuffing bombs inside turduckens set to go off at Easter. They had a fallin' out and...You know, over there in I-ran and I-raq and I-rabia they chop off heads and hands and whatnots just for the fun of it."

"Are you sayin' you think Charlene Lehough chopped up Virgil Carter for fun?"

"Well, could be her who did it, or someone else. I never reckoned for one second it would have been your mama who killed some gal named Zander, like Maximo still thinks is the case."

Hmmm? "Here's a semi-hot tip for you Chief Potter," she said. "I have received, uh, anonymous rumors that Butch Bernard might be up to mischief in his mama's garage."

"Butch Bernard! Heck, that's the young fella my boy, Roy, has been hangin' out with lately," the Chief said, starting for the door. "I'll look into the matter and find out if they've been smokin' marijuana cigarettes or somethin'."

Henrietta had seen right away how that dead body over in the State Police lab could be the remains of Virgil Carter. After getting out of the hospital down in Texas, Virgil would have had reason to chase Charlene Lehough to Okmulgee County with payback in mind. According to Maximo Morgan, she had broke his skull with the butt of a shotgun, so according to her own self,

Henrietta reckoned Charlene probably got the best of him again. Not because she had become a "black widow spider" sent from overseas—which would be a big story alright, dang it—but because of love turned to hate in another same old story about an ordinary marital spat getting out of hand. And dog gone it, just like the earlier vice versa notion of Maximo Morgan's—that Virgil murdered Charlene for the same reason—she now realized she was not onto much of a whodunnit after all.

Hmmm? After thinking about the matter for awhile longer, Henrietta came up with a notion about Professor Lehough's recent strange behavior. She got on her eye-phone, looked up the number for the Casbah Club up in Okmulgee and punched in a call. Miss Xander was to return there tonight by popular demand, but...In answer to her asking an assistant club manager about the scheduled time of the strip-teaser's appearance on stage, he said: "We cancelled that no-good no-show. Got a better one of Little Egypt's daughters—Beautifuler! Buxomer! Bolder!—to do a hotter hoochie-coochie tonight. You gotta see fab-u-lous Fatima crawl on her belly like a rep-tile, wiggled straight out of the Nile River just last week. You will not believe she has a bone in her back when you see her dance the..."

After he had finished his spiel, she asked about the reason for Miss Xander's no-show. "The little snake gave none," the assistant manager said. "In fact, she hasn't had the decency to take a call or answer one since going off stage two weeks ago. But put this in the paper: The fab-u-lous Fatima is Beautifuler! Buxomer! Bolder! and crawls on her belly like..."

Hmmm? Maximo Morgan, a private detective likely to get a thing or two right, was still accusing Wynona Sue of being tangled up in a love triangle involving Professor Lehough and another woman named Zander, spelled with a Z, he thought.

Now the professor's wife, Charlene, had come back from overseas wearing a radicalized burka. Xander, spelled with an X hailed from someplace over there called Algiers. Hmmm? Henrietta put off calling her mother to tell the "good" news about Professor Lehough's wife being back to life. Though she tried to resist, a notion came to her that both Charlene Lehough and Wynona Sue had hard feelings toward Virgil Carter, and maybe Xander did too. Both Wynona Sue and Charlene also seemed to suffer from love turned to hate for Professor Lehough, which also might be the case of Xander's frame of mind. If they got into cahoots…

Hmmm? Henrietta couldn't help herself from thinking of the three gals—Charlene, Xander, and her own dang mother—as characters in a big news story headlined either ***BLACK WIDOW SPIDERS DEVOUR LOVER AFTER WHOOPEE!*** or maybe ***WITCHES MAKE DEVILISH PROFESSOR DISAPPEAR!***

Thirty-Six

Max lounged on a bench outside a State Police building in Oklahoma City, munching a tuna fish sandwich while waiting for a team of crime lab bureaucrats to officially identify the body he had personally brought from the crime scene three days ago. They refused to let him stay in the cooler with the corpse. Obviously didn't want a pro looking over their shoulders when they finally got around to carving it up. Yesterday they even muscled him out of the building lobby, and told him to stay out. He had a hunch something fishy was going on. That was the way it sometimes went with civil servants who seemed to think slicing-and-dicing cases of murrr-derrr was a nine-to-five lay. Two rooms at the Holiday Inn—for him and his mother—was getting to be expensive. Room service shut down at eleven. Luckily, he had stumbled upon the R&J Supper Club, his kind of late night joint: Cheezy with a capital C. The mac-and-cheddar souffle was, as they say, to die for, but also pricy.

And all for what? In his gut, he already knew the victim—lying on a cold slab inside the State Police morgue, rotting like a beached mackerel—was a vamp named...His cell phone buzzed. It was Potter calling.

"Maximo, I wanted you to be the first, uh, one of the first to know: Case closed. Two days ago we found out..."

"Let me guess: Charlene Lehough showed up a-livvve, right?"

"Yeah, uh, right. How'd you know?"

"Had the runaway adulteress angle figured out threeee days ago. Simple shamus work."

"Gee, I wish you'da passed along the information. We've about bankrupted the town dredging Lake Henryetta; and spent Sunday night diving for Mrs. Lehough's head and, uh other body parts. Now we have to hire someone to bulldoze all the junk back into the reservoir."

Max cut-off the call. Potter a bureaucrat in police uniform was what he called a do-nutter, the kind of guy who wore the badge only for the goodies that went along with it. The phony Five-O had refused to collar the strawberry blonde hairdresser. Probably he'd not yet even gotten around to grilling Professor Lehough about the lethal love triangle involving him, Wyyynona Suuue and Zannn-derrr. Max himself had doped out that Charlene Lehough was not a victim of murrr-derr on Sunday, when he dropped by the house to pick up his mother on the way to Oklahoma City. Mom was crying. Kasannndra Kardassshian was laughing. "Max, forget about the 'Case of a Tramp Named Charlene'," the dame said, which was suspicious. "I am not a natural blonde. I am a brunette." More suspicious. "Specifically, my name is Charlene Lehough, and your name is..." he'd expected her to say "Trouble with a capital T," but..."Hopeless with a capital H," she said. "Just notarize my signature on this piece of paper and leave me alone."

That was the was the way the cookie almost always crumbled

in the personal life of a private Richarrrd. Like the doll in the *Case of Final Curtain*, Sandy was carrying a torch for him bright enough to read by. Splitting was for the best. Theirs had to be a passing affair. Hopeless. So he had stamped her Jane Henry and put her back on the street. Keeping mum about it had at least given the frightened philly a head start on getting away from her mannn trouble with Virgil Carrr-terrr. Like Mike said in the *Case of To Bury a Friend*, private gumshoe work was a ball, yeah, all crime, women and song. A private dick had to be hardboiled when it came to dames.

Looking back on their bittersweet farewell, the *Case of Kiss Me Deadly* came to mind. "You have only one real lasting love," a skirt said to Mike. "Now who could that be?" he asked. Her answer, plain and simple as a ham sandwich: "You." That was just the way it was in the personal life of a private...Another line from the case came knocking, this one a word of advice delivered by Mike's secretary and main squeeze, Velda. "First you find a little thread, the little thread leads to a string, the string leads to a rope, and from the rope you hang by the neck. What kind of girl was she?" Always a good question. Almost never with a good an-swerrr.

Max mentally followed Velda's tip backwards to the beginning of his own *Case of The Jealous Strawberry Blonde*, when he'd come close to putting his head in a noose. Slowly, he began to work his way inch by inch back up the rope. What a sap he'd been to believe the strawberry blonde doll just happened to drop by his Mr. Quickie cubicle to get a Notary Public stamp. And just happened to notice his private gumshoe plaque. Acting hesitant as a virgin at first, but then admitting to mannn trouble a little too quickly. Referring to her boyfriend's piece of strange on the side as a hissing cockroach tipped him to the hard edge she tried to hide, but he had let it slide. The innocent-seeming babe conned him to nose around, ask questions, tail Zander, maybe get spotted in a compromising situation. Yeah, the conniving kitten set him up to take the fall for murrr-derrr of the "other woman" that would allow her—otherwise the most likely suspect—to skate the rap. And it almost worked.

Max climbed another inch, recalling his close call on the front porch of Lehough's bungalow: Charleeene or Zannn-derrr, inside with the professor, must have heard something. Something such as Wyyynona Suuue on the prowwwl. The lights went off. If he'd not faded just in time, yeah, next would have a come a gunnn-shot, and him clomping from the murrr-derrr scene with a guilty looking egg on his face.

Getting from rope to string, Max's hamster-like mind spun back to his next encounter with the wily Wyyynona Suuue at the Chair Crushers Cafe. Realizing by then that she had picked the wrong chump to frame for murrr-derrr, the conniving canary changed her tune. "To heck with him," she'd said about her cheating fiance, "let's have a real date." Tried to make him believe she wasn't as green with jealousy as Central Park grass, that her "classic love story" was only a "funny comedy." Bad break for her that he happened to get a call from the lawyer, Willis, asking him to track down a runaway adulteress, who happened to be Lehough's wife! When he put the conniving killer wise to her flim-flamming fiance's prior legal engagement, she lost her cool. And no doubt lost interest in rubbing out Zannn-derrr, though only until the wife, Charlene Lehough, went misss-ing. Another bad break for her that his investigation of the presumed death of the tramp named Charlene led him to open a case with her own hair and face colors painted on it in bold type: *STRAWBERRY BLONDE*, green with *JEALOUSY!*

Max inched onto the thread of his case. Before fingering Wyyynona Suuue for the murrr-derrr of Zannn-derrr, he'd liked her for doer of the doing in of the runaway adulteress, Charleeene Lee-hooough. Same scenario: love triangle. Same motive: jealousy. Same old story. Tailing the hot-tempered tomato, he'd watched her break into her two-timing lover's darkened digs. He'd eyeballed another figure skulking in the noir outside. He'd witnessed the saucy seductress come out, dragging a large bag, then take the skulker's a/k/a Zannn-derrr's body to her kitchen, for butch-errring. Unfortunately, though still staked out on Trudgeon Street, he had nodded off. Chances were the bloodthirsty babe lost her appetite and found that her garbage disposal wasn't up to finishing the job. So while he was snoozing, obviously she hauled Zannn-derrr's remains—whittled down to just a torso by then—to the lake for a deeeep dive. Too bad for her he'd already put Potter to work, dredging.

With Charlene Lehough now known to be topside, by simple process of bloody e-lim-in-aaation, the body lying in a State Police frozen meat case like a butchered halibut had to be the other dame, Zannn-derrr. The *Case of The Jealous Strawberry Blonde* was sewn up tight as a hooker's purrrse. Only a single remaining detail…Max's phone buzzed. Potter again. What now?

"Hey, Maximo, you cut me off," the slow footed flatfoot said. "I wanted to tell you that I went to see Professor Lehough, just to check on your suspicions about Wynona Sue and him bein' in some kind of love triangle with someone called 'Zander' who you're so sure is…Have they identified that body you took over there yet?"

"Spill it, Pat. What did Lehough cop to when you gave him the third degreeee?"

"He said 'Zander' was his own self, a sorta nickname from high school, short for Alexander."

Hmmmm?

"So, Maximo, I know you mean good, but...but, I am hereby ordering you to butt out of police investigation of that dead body over there and leave it to us professionals."

Max cut him off again. Mike and police Captain Pat Chambers had run-ins with one another from time to time, almost always about Pat wanting to play by the book and Mike not ever in the mood to curl up by the fire and read when there was murrr-derrr to be dealt with by whatever means nec-ess-arry. In the *Case of The Girl Hunters,* believing that his honey, Velda, had been killed, Mike hit the bottle, hard. Pat, believing that Mike was responsible for Velda's demise, beat him up, bad. But when Velda turned up alive in the sequel *Case of The Snake*, they buried the hatchet. Potter was no Pat Chambers and likely never would live up to the name, but . .

"Hey, you, Morgan!" someone shouted. A guy wearing a bloody smock stood at the doorway of the State Police building. Max got up from the bench, put the remains of a second tuna fish sandwich in the pocket of his trench coat and ankled over to him. The lab tech handed him a couple of sheets of paper and said, "Here's your autopsy report, and your bill for services rendered."

"Enough DNA for you to make a positive I.D.?"

"Oh yeah, almost sixty pounds, big for a Flathead."

"Flat?" Lab lingo for the unfortunately "headless" condition of a murrr-derr victim sounded harsh, even to the ear of a hardboiled P.I.

"Yep, your murrr-derrr victim is a catfish."

"'Fisssh'? As in seeea-food?"

"Are you hard of hearing? Catfish! Now, pull your car around back and take the stinking thing off our hands."

Oh well, in the words of the ever memorable Billy Desloge in *Case of A Deadly Deal at the Red Dog Casino*, sometimes private dicking was like "drawing easy to the inside after a long slow squeeze," and in this case unluckily failing to come up with a queen of hearts to fill a royal flush. He'd had a hunch that "Zander" might be a term for a fish after looking up the word in a dictionary, but…His cell phone buzzed. It was Potter again. No doubt the town clown was calling to bury a hatchet and ask for help with a new case of possibly murrr-derrr.

"Maximo! This just in: Charlene Lehough casted a laughing spell, grabbed a copper's gun and ran off, screaming! She's armed and mad as a wet hen at…"

"Let me guess. The dame's on the warpath against her estranged husband, the professor, right? Divorrrce lit-ig-aaation almost always leads to murrr-derrr."

"No, she screamed it's you she's out to get, for…."

"Oh yeah? Let me guess. For seeing through her Kasandra Kardashian alias, no doubt."

"No, they say it was when she prised open a metal box in her lawyer's office that she went crazy. Contents of the box proved to be…"

"Let me guess," said Max. The line from the *Case of the Maltese Falcon* came to mind.

"Pots and pans," said Potter.

"Yeah, the stuff that dreams are made of," said Max.

Hmmm?

The Case of The Jabberwock next came to Max's mind. His first murrr-derrr mystery, read to him by his mother back when she still hoped he would turn out to be a girl. Still a stumper.

"Something killed someone," Little Alice from Wonderland said, "that much is clear, at any rate." Or was it, "Someone killed something"? Hmmm? Max held off mentally closing the *Case of The Jealous Strawberry Blonde.* Wyyynona Suuue was the kind of dame they call a *femme fatale* alright, Cajun-speak for a doll deadly as a black widow spider. If his client once removed, Alexander "Zander" Lehough, didn't protect himself in the clinches and fight off her wily woman's ways of luring him into her web, Max had a hunch murrr-derrr would soon be in the noir. And the Fat Mannnnn was hardly ever wrong.

Thirty-Seven

On a day in her life she could hardly believe could ever have come, Henrietta woke up with a plan of escape to a brighter future. Soon as Mr. Harold got back to town, she was going to quit her *Weekly Herald* job; move to a big city where nobody knew her; work as a cafe waitress if need be; and get a boyfriend. The only reason she dropped out of college five years ago and came back to her little ol' hometown that she'd been named for was to care for her ailing mother and now...Henrietta sighed. Looking after Wynona Sue would not be her chore no more. The time had come for her to get on the backside of bad weather, move on out into the world around her and see what happened.

Heck, Virgil Carter, an ordinary pots and pans salesman with prior unseemly associations in his past almost got elected to be Vice-President of the United States. And he was not only still alive, but back to being famous. Though now he was black-haired, wore glasses and a mustache, she had recognized Virgil last night on the *Jimmy Kimmel Live!* TV show from Hollywood, promoting *Everlasting Leadware* as "guaranteed to outlive you," and handy for folks to have around---- not just for cooking—in case they happened to get a fractured skull. She wouldn't be surprised to next see that Butch Bernard and Roy Potter also got to be famous for their line of *Skin & Bone Soul Mates*. Same for the "Xander" gal she had tracked down, who turned out to be an ordinary daughter of a dentist in Okmulgee—named Doris Ann Haggard—who had "disappeared" for awhile only to get a boob job. Already she was back to dancing the hoochie-coochie at the Casbah Club and on her first night earned more in tips than she used to get throwed at her in a week. There was no reason she her own self couldn't do just as good, Henrietta reckoned. But first she had to get to the office, take her final college exam and put this week's edition of the *Weekly Herald* to bed.

At her work desk fifteen minutes later, she opened her laptop and nervously waited for Professor LeRoy's final exam to come by email. Though she had studied up on all the classic love stories, and wracked her brain in particular about the one by William Shakespeare titled *Othello*, for the life of her own self she couldn't see how the dark-skinned Moor general killing the love of his life—even if she was only his anima—was a classic love story. No gal would even think of doing such a thing to her own soul mate, she reckoned, except Wynona Sue who had got so mad at Professor Lehough for him giving her the mitten. Henrietta her own self had never wished Gaylord Goodhart would come to any harm worse than, say, a broken neck. Hopefully the final exam would be a list of True-or-False questions about classic tales of passion, jealousy and hate that would give her a fifty-fifty chance of passing and maybe even...*Ping!*

Uh oh.

Professor LeRoy:

My eleventh grade English teacher, Mrs. Tuck, required us to write a paper on a well known, seemingly paradoxical passage of poetry—the mournful wail of a man condemned to hang for killing his significant other—and I have wrestled with it ever since in the context of studying the mystery of the classic love story. Now I pass on the puzzler to each of you, from The Ballad of Reading Gaol by Oscar Wilde, to-wit:

Yet each man kills the thing he loves,
By each let this be heard,
Some do it with a bitter look,
Some with a flattering word,
The coward does it with a kiss,
The brave man with a sword!
Some kill their love when they are young,
And some when they are old;
Some strangle with the hands of Lust,
Some with the hands of Gold:
The kindest use a knife, because
The dead so soon grow cold.

Post comment of two-hundred words or less by 6:00 p.m. today. (Please comment on content only, not Oscar's sexual orientation. Nor on any perceived homophobia or other political incorrectness on my part. Pretty please, with vanilla ice cream on top.)

What in tarnation? Henrietta, clueless, looked at her watch. In addition to getting the paper ready for printing, she had to be at the town hall bail-posting room that afternoon to see her mother get put in "bracelets and a collar" before she could even think about writing a comment on the paradox poem. Frantically, she typed: ***CHIEF POTTER CLEARS SON AND ACCOMPLICE OF MURDER SUSPICION /***

Police Chief Potter yesterday warned that whoever started a rumor that his boy, Roy, and a friend, Butch "Walter" Bernard, were hatchet murderers will be arrested if identified. "The young men have done nothing wrong by upgrading a robot into a humanoid," the proud father said. "'Henrietta' is a mostly metal soul mate for an old man in Japan." The humanoid ----named Henrietta with an i instead of a y, but probably in honor of the town—is partly made of realistic 3-D prints of a skull and hand bones put together by Roy Potter, then covered with varnished catfish skin glued on by Butch "Walter" Bernard. "She" is programmed to talk to a Mr. Ito like an oldtime movie seductress and to move her arms and hands in certain ways to please the elderly Japanese man. Her inventors plan to roll out clones for the local market in time for the upcoming prom and wedding seasons.

Henrietta looked at her watch again. Dang it, she had tried to convince Wynona Sue it was bad luck to count chickens before setting on eggs, but her mother was bound and determined to have the ending of her classic love story put down in tomorrow's paper, no matter what. So...***WYNONA SUE HEBERT nee O'HARA WEDS /***

Wynona Sue Hebert nee O'Hara of Trudgeon Street marched down an aisle in the town hall Justice of the Peace room yesterday to marry the love of her life, Professor Alexander "Zander" Lehough of Division Street. The bride wore a long white Cinderella dress that she got on sale from the online Disney store. Underneath a lacy veil, her face was no doubt made up to look good by her co-beauticians at The Best Little Hair House in Town.

Henrietta paused, but then decided not to mention that E-Z Mart had again run out of real flowers, as well as bean burritos, and went back to writing up her mother's would-be wedding:

The bride carried a bouquet of artificial red carnations. A boom box played her favorite old classical song called "Isn't She Lovely," sung by an Irish tenor named Steven Wonder. Her daughter from a previously brief and unhappy marriage, Henrietta Hebert, serving as Maid of Honor, stood next to a podium. As did the groom, standing also by a cardboard box containing a broke-legged hissing pet cockroach from Madagascar named Mickey, grinning from ear to ear like a…

Henrietta looked up to see, of all people, the professor his own self; already all shined up for the wedding but looking unsteady on his feet and glum as a prisoner locked up in that old paradoxial reading gaol, about to be hanged. To judge by his bloodshot eyes, Henrietta reckoned the would-be groom had been either over indulging in a strong spiritous beverage, or maybe weeping. "I, uh, think, well, that it's only right and proper that some, uh, mention be made of, uh, Ann," he mumbled, handing to her a scrap of paper. "If you would be kind enough to put this in the *Weekly Herald*, I would be grateful."

Ann? Doris Ann? Doris Ann Haggard? What in tarnation? Henrietta read what the professor had wrote:

> ***Lehough, A.*** *– age unknown, died February 29, 2016.*
> *Cause of death: A mystery. Services extremely private.*

Hmmm?

THE

END

64226344R00145

Made in the USA
Charleston, SC
20 November 2016